CROSS THE BORDER—
CLOSE THE GAP

Cross the Border— Close the Gap

LESLIE A. FIEDLER

STEIN AND DAY / *Publishers* / New York

First published in 1972
Copyright © 1971 by Leslie A. Fiedler
Library of Congress Catalog Card No. 72-81822
All rights reserved
Published simultaneously in Canada by Saunders of Toronto Ltd
Printed in the United States of America
Stein and Day/*Publishers*/7 East 48 Street, New York, N.Y. 10017
ISBN 0-8128-1479-7

Contents

Acknowledgments

The author wishes to thank the editors and publishers of the following, under whose imprints parts of this book originally appeared:

ENCOUNTER for "The Middle Against Both Ends," August, 1955.

NEW YORK HERALD TRIBUNE MAGAZINE for "The Death of Avant-Garde Literature," May 17, 1964.

ODYSSEY PRESS for "In Quest of George Lippard," first published as an Introduction to *Quaker City*, 1970.

PLAYBOY for "Cross the Border—Close the Gap," December, 1969.

SHOW for "A Night with Mr. Teas," October, 1961.

CROSS THE BORDER—
CLOSE THE GAP

Introduction

As THE TWENTIETH CENTURY enters its eighth decade and I myself move on into my sixth, it becomes ever more apparent that I, like all other literary survivors of "Modernism," whether poets, dramatists, novelists, or critics, must come to terms with the death of that movement. Still seemingly immortal during my own youth, it survived neither that youth nor the second Great War which climaxed it; but its metaphorical demise passed unnoticed at first among the real deaths of millions of real men and women. Since 1955, however, no one has been able to doubt that the movement represented in its declining years by Pound and Eliot and Valéry, as well as by Proust and Mann and Joyce, is dead and gone—leaving to its heirs (who can never be sure they are not also its murderers) an obligation to graveside oratory. Some mourn aloud; some pretend to indifference; others frankly and openly rejoice as at a deliverance. But I am moved to do none of them, willing ever to let the dead bury the dead and glad only that I am not among them. Instead I have, as the following essays bear witness, felt obligated rather to prophesy what will come next—attempting in a score of ways, all tentative and profoundly ambivalent, to surmise the character and probable destiny of the movement for which there is still no better name than Post-Modernism.

To deal with that new movement, quite obviously it will be necessary to develop a really new criticism, free of all vestiges of the elitism and the Culture Religion which still obsessed our immediate predecessors. I have, therefore, become more and more interested in the kinds of books with which such elitist approaches have had the most difficulty in dealing—turning from the Modernist canon of

3

subtle and difficult works whose readers could scarcely help feeling themselves chosen as well as few to the kind of books which no one has ever congratulated himself on being able to read: books which join together all possible audiences, children and adults, women and men, the sophisticated and the naïve. And in pursuit of such works, I have been willing to cross the border which once separated High Art from Pop.

I am convinced that criticism at the moment can no longer condescend to popular literature as, in fact, my own earlier criticisn did; that it must resist all impulses to create hierarchies, even those implicit in what seem harmless distinctions of genre or medium. For this reason, the reader will discover jumbled together in this volume reflections on movies, comic books, on pop songs and Japanese woodblock prints, as well as more traditional analyses of novels and poems—which is to say, will perceive that I do my best not to reject those works of art whose muse is a machine and whose fate seems more closely linked to the history of Technology than that of the Spirit. He will further perceive that I have concentrated on the mythic element in all of these, which is to say, on an element which is indifferent to medium, rather than on those formal elements which distinguish one medium from another.

I am quite aware that there is a kind of politics implicit in the critical position I take in these essays, a populist, even anarchist stance based on an impatience with all distinctions of kind created on the analogy of a class-structured society. I feel myself more and more pressed these days toward the position so outrageously expressed by Tolstoi in his essay *What is Art?* I am still resisting the temptation, however, finally to embrace the point of view which urges that the only art worth preserving and praising is the art which joins all men together at their deepest and simplest level of response. In fairness to my own past and my own work as a novelist and poet, I feel it necessary to retain still a respect for traditional high art. Nonetheless, I grow more and more uncomfortably aware that the cult based on the appreciation of works available only to a few has proved not only repressive in a political sense, but even more damaging in a psychological one.

If I live long enough, perhaps I shall finally grow young enough to disavow all vestiges of the humanistic tradition that persist in my thinking—turning my back on the past, recent and remote, quite as if, like some fifteen-year-old, I, too, inhabit a world I never made. The truth is that I feel myself in such an alien world, having been reborn for the second time in my life some five or six years ago and being therefore very young, indeed. Like many in my generation, I have been *thrice* born—first into radical dissent, then into radical disillusion and the fear of innocence, finally into whatever it is that lies beyond both commitment and disaffection. This means that for me the model of Dionysus no longer works, since he was only twice born: once of the Mother, the next time of the Father. What remains, I suppose, is to dare—without mythological precedent—to be born of one's own children.

In any case, the reader should be aware that this volume of my essays is among the products of my third birth, as the earlier volumes are of my second; my original innocence is recorded in print nowhere at all, since I have never published anything I wrote before the age of thirty. My first book (retrospectively called *An End to Innocence*) appeared, in fact, as I was approaching the close of the fourth decade of my life, so that I have felt free with the passage of years to invent and live into a youth which belongs not to history but to myth, not to fact, but to my dreams. Somewhere in his letter Mark Twain casually observes that he had never dreamed himself anything but a young man, and I suspect this is true of all of us. But this is a way of saying, is it not, that however far we may have progressed past innocence in our waking lives, once asleep we revert to that pristine state of innocence which apparently did not, cannot end once and for all. That innocence we are continually beginning to end.

ONE

Some Notes on Ukiyoe:
A Word on the History of Taste and
Three Dissenting Opinions

I AM GRATEFUL to Mr. Michener's book* for two reasons: first, because it is high time that there be a popular book by an American on an art which is both popular and (in a real though secondary sense) American; and second, because I have been long waiting for an occasion to say something about an art form that has moved and shaped me in a way to which I find it hard to do justice. From about the time of the Restoration of the Stuarts to the beginning of our own Civil War, a group of middle-class Japanese painters, who did not consider themselves artists in any serious sense of the word, produced for mass distribution what they called *ukiyoe* or floating world pictures, which possess, accidentally, as it were, the merits of high art. These pictures have in common a technique and a subject matter; they are printed from wood blocks in several colors and portray (more than three-quarters of them at any rate) popular actors and well-known prostitutes—or, as the Japanese prefer to say, *bijin*, "beautiful persons." They are, in a word, pin-ups.

It is difficult for such pictures, which are neither singular examples of technique nor portrayals of traditional subjects, to find honor inside of their own culture. Especially in Japan, where one by one the arts, the skills, the sports—the very looking at a maple leaf or drinking a cup of tea—have been subsumed under the contempla-

---

* James A. Michener, *The Floating World*.

7

tive ideals of Zen Buddhism, where everything to be thought worthy had to be rethought in terms of eternity, it is nearly impossible to take seriously so resolutely secular an art. Only sex in Japan has remained a matter of fact; for in that culture, the attempt so basic to our own to religify sex and sexualize religion has not, so far as I know, ever been made; and *ukiyoe* are, as we shall see, fundamentally sexual.

Even yet, most qualified Japanese will not grant *ukiyoe* to be an art at all. As an *art,* it was invented from certain examples which happened to survive—twice over: once by the French "decadents" of the end of the nineteenth century; and once by rich Americans intent on making us truly the heirs of all the ages. To the "decadents" (I use the Continental name rather than our more honorific word "symbolists" to help make the point), there was in these prints a whiff of something at once delicate and corrupt, nonrealistic and sexual, which they confused with the newly rehabilitated pre-Raphaelites, certain contemporary tendencies in painting, etc. Those epicene, barely adolescent little dishes of Harunobu, for instance, they blended in their own minds with the Virgins of Fra Angelico, making that hash of titillation and religiosity which tickled them.

As for the American millionaires, they were apparently delighted to find a style at once so exotic and congenial. *Ukiyoe* is, of course, bourgeois and open—the most undifficult and human of the Oriental arts. One has to think only of the way in which the human figure is annihilated by symbolic nature and space in a Zen painting and compare it with the way the face of a pretty girl possesses the whole area of a *ukiyoe* print to get the point. In addition, the prints were relatively cheap; and the sense of getting a bargain, of buying at the lowest rate what its owners do not know to be a treasure, attracts the businessman even out of hours. The Japanese soon caught on, to be sure, upping the prices and producing the excellent counterfeits of which our museums are full; but meanwhile the decisive moment was past. The handbills and souvenirs of the red-light district of eighteenth-century Tokyo were well on the way to becoming an art of the American museum.

The moment at which *ukiyoe* as a living form disappears is the moment of the opening of Japan by the American fleet. This art, which must have seemed another country to the Japanese officially closed off during its life to all other countries, is ready to hand when America begins the attempt to assimilate culturally what it has inherited politically. Along with the garishness of Chinese Manchu art, it is the Orientalism easiest to come to terms with at a time when Orientalism was becoming the keynote of American acquisitive interior decorating. From the interiors of Beacon Street, *ukiyoe* found its way into the museums of Boston and westward from there along the main lines of Chautauqua culture. At any rate, for better or worse (and astonishingly, it is for better), America possesses at the moment the largest collections of Japanese prints anywhere.

Sufficient unto these collections is Mr. Michener's book. For my taste it is in spots a little offhand and breezy, sometimes popularizing rather than popular; but it is informative and enthusiastic —a labor of love, its scholarship, as far as I can tell, scrupulous. My sole large objection, and it is a very large one, is to the quality of the reproductions, which are abominable in every regard. The colors are so poor that reference from textual comment to reproduction often leaves one utterly confused, the famous sensitive line blurred and broken.

I do not, of course, agree with all of Mr. Michener's judgments and explanations; and I should like to register three special dissents, based on a taste and a method of interpretation quite different from his own. "Therefore *ukiyoe*. . .," Mr. Michener says at one point, "was a religious word carrying strong Buddhist overtones; the sad, floating, evanescent, grief-stricken world. . . . A less appropriate title for the kinds of pictures we shall meet in this book would be difficult to devise." This is hard even to understand, much less agree with. Mr. Michener could scarcely deny that the world of *ukiyoe*—the world of entertainers paring their toenails, rouging their lips, hurriedly suckling babies between customers, or watching in mirrors the comb passing through the curtain of hair before their hidden face—is a world of vanity. Perhaps he only intends to say that it is hardly a "grief-stricken" world, that its proper tone is a joy which does not even imagine, much less contemplate fearfully, a tomorrow. But the painters in the backrooms of brothels knew the half-world in which they lived: the cages outside of the houses in which the girls were displayed, the guards at the gates of the district to keep them from escaping the realm of "pleasure." There is a melancholy, a nuance of sickly sweet disgust behind their bright flat patterns, the sparkle of their mica backgrounds. One cannot scrupulously follow the month to month shift of fashionable hair-dos (so that experts date the prints from the changing coiffures), or shift subject as popular preference shifts from beauty to beauty, without acquiring some awareness of the treachery of sense and time.

But there is more than this. The two great compulsive themes of *ukiyoe* are the prostitute and the actor, the paid simulator of pleasure and the paid performer of rage and grief; and these archetypes, these living reminders of the difference between "seems" and "is" give the Japanese print a metaphysical dimension. The actor prints especially present simulation *in depth,* being counterfeits in ink and paper of an actor imitating a puppet imitating a human being (for such is *kabuki,* the dramatic art the printmakers exploited). To this subject matter the manner of *ukiyoe* perfectly corresponds.

It is, at first glance, all manner, a mannerist art. Mr. Michener quite properly protests against the older moralizing histories of *ukiyoe* which presented this fact as a condemnation of *ukiyoe,* a revelation of its "decadence." But though his individual judgment of merit differs from those of the moralists, his understanding of what mannerism in general is remains the same as theirs; and he fails to get their essential point or to see them in terms of the non-Japanese art they most resemble. *Ukiyoe* not declines into but begins with distortion and device: the trifling with point of view, the search for effect. And the neck of an impossible Utomaro woman is extended in the same way and for the same reasons as that of the infamous "Virgin of the Long Neck" of Parmagianino.

But we know now the metaphysics to which such distortion aspires, and we do not despise an Utomaro any more than a Tintoretto or an El Greco. The mannerism of the Japanese is not like ours learned or mystical; but the printmakers who learn to show in a single print a woman's face through her hair, behind a fan or a screen and in a mirror; who illuminate one scene from three different sources of light; who study the human body and its distortion at the point where, say, a foot passes from air into water; soon discover that, whatever their intent, they have invented a language for discoursing on appearance and reality.

The key symbol of *ukiyoe* is the mirror: the maiden bent to her glass to discover the illusion which is her face—or the wild girl peering through the tangle of her hair into the pool caught in the hollow of a rock. "Vanity, vanity!" is the text; and we do not need the scallops of cloud that Harunobu and others use for the upper frames of their pictures to tell us conventionally that all this, too, shall pass away.

"One is struck by certain similarities between the fate of *ukiyoe* in Japan and the state of poetry in America. Each was once a popular art. . . . Each became sterile and died for the lack of vital new ideas. Belatedly . . . the reborn art had to be content with an esoteric existence." Wrong again—wrong on all counts. Poetry was, of course, never a popular art, in any meaning of that word; and insofar as it died at all, died precisely because it sought to become one. The comparison proper to *ukiyoe* is not with a formal and traditional art of any kind, but with the movies, with the comics, with television, and jazz.

"Popular" is too ambiguous a word to trust; for two of its commonest meanings are middlebrow and folk. But *ukiyoe* is lowbrow and urban—a mass-produced art of the city. Like all other mass arts, its rise is coincident with the development of a new mechanical device which makes possible mass production. The cases of the movies and television are obvious; and even jazz could not become generally accepted before the perfection of cheap phonograph recordings. The invention which made *ukiyoe* possible was *kento,* a reliable system of guides to insure perfect superimposition of several color blocks.

The Japanese print, it must be pointed out, is not a wood-block engraving in our usual understanding of the term; it is a strange enough thing in all conscience: the mechanical reproduction of a drawing that never existed outside of a shorthand indication. Like all the mass arts, it is not only antigenteel and antisentimental, but also without any consciousness of itself as art—and therefore quite content to be produced on the assembly line. And yet somehow the original conception of the artist manages to survive the engraver, the printer and the publisher; for the wood block on which the latter collaborate is not a medium but a means of distribution.

It is hard to see even any change in the conventions of drawing brought about by the transition from painting to printings. The single exception may be the matter of line, which began as the thick, modulated stroke of the writing brush and was thinned in time into a penlike sensitivity. The trend is from abstraction to representation, from (in the case of the *bijin)* calligraphy to pornography. In the beginning, the outlines of the female figure are almost Chinese characters for woman; in the end, they respond sensitively to the current conventions of sexual attractiveness.

Most important of all, the mass art begins not as ritual, but as "entertainment," which is to say, as titillation wrapped as a commodity in a secularized world. If it becomes high art, it must do so secretly, behind the backs of its consumers and even sometimes of its creators. Its mere popularity is not hopelessly inimical to seriousness, but it is discouraging; and certainly it stands in the way of the critics who find it hard to consider such work seriously. It requires a peculiar sort of sophistication to go in search of excellence in Krazy Kat or Charlie Chaplin or Louis Armstrong; and the Japanese did not themselves develop such a sophistication. It required the intervention of American appreciators to make the leap, in a way not unlike that in which French musicologists had to lead the way to serious analysis of our own jazz.

It is the hopeful lesson of *ukiyoe* that even the most mechanical and debased demand for "entertainment" can stir into life a true art and that such an art can manage to get by in a society which fundamentally despises it. But it is also the lesson of *ukiyoe* that such an art quite quickly exhausts its meager resources, and, being forbidden real experimentation, cannot renew itself. The modern attempts of a few Japanese to redeem this lapsed mass art on an "esoteric" level suggest to me not Eliot or Pound, whom Mr. Michener's comparison seems intended to evoke, but the not quite convincing, middlebrow efforts of a Gershwin or a Brubeck.

"Anyone familiar with western art who studies the prints reproduced in this book must conclude that one of the striking characteristics of *ukiyoe* is its freedom from erotic content. *Ukiyoe* avoids nakedness and foregoes slick suggestiveness." Of the four *ukiyoe* prints I myself own, one is a triple print by Utamaro showing a group of abalone fisherwomen in varying degrees of nakedness; the second a study of a nude stepping into her bath by Harunobu; the third, also by Utamaro, the head and upper torso of a girl from "one of the six best houses," fully clothed to be sure; and the fourth an anonymous piece of hopeful pornography showing an ancient gentleman with a grotesquely oversized phallus addressing himself rather dreamily to a *bijin,* whose face is all calm and submission. Both the old gentleman and the girl are fully dressed except for adjustments necessary to their sport. It is only in this latter sense that *ukiyoe* "avoids nakedness."

Even excluding the simple pornography of which my last item is an example, one could assemble an interesting and worthy collection of nudes and quasi-nudes from the masters of *ukiyoe.* It is a subject which intrigued not only Utamaro and Harunobu but even the more "classical" Koryusai. In an art which so desperately sought to render texture without shading, one would expect a concern with the contrast of silk and flesh, the bare breast falling out of the kimono, etc. The Japanese printmaker is almost always averse to showing mere nakedness, to be sure; even in my Harunobu print, where the girl is quite nude, her kimono hangs on a screen behind her. The point is the opposite of what it may seem. For the Japanese, the folds of the kimono itself, the constriction of the obi, the formalization of the female which denies the mere natural curves of the body is more erotic that the blatant display of nakedness.

It is easy enough to say that the nudes in the triple Utamaro are merely working girls, stripped for their trade—but why this concern with their trade? I remember quite well the Japanese who sold it to me asserting with a sly grin that this was a "spring picture," a term that I did not then understand, but which I have learned since means simply pornography. Of course, it was all in part salesmanship—this appeal to the barbarian; but there was, too, a conviction that nudeness portrayed under any pretext was aimed at provocation. The distinction between the "dirty book," which Mr. Michener tells us took almost half the time of the greatest talents of *ukiyoe,* and their other work is not nearly so great as he assumes.

From the lower left-hand corner of my Harunobu, a little green frog looks directly upward into the unseen shadow of the raised leg of the bather about to get into the tub. He is the symbol of the springtime in a hundred poems, of the Buddhist awakening to a new life; and the leap he signifies in this secular study is a gentle and melancholy parody of spiritual rebirth. But my clothed Utamaro beauty is the most voluptuous of all, though all her hidden body must be declared by her face; the slit eyes, the willow eyebrows, but especially the outrageously cruel and tiny mouth with the stiff curled prong of its protruding tongue.

Even the actors who constitute the second great theme of *ukiyoe* are essentially erotic objects, whether the frail players of female parts with their epicene charm or the great, virile lady-killers of legend—their front hair shaved off according to the law that sought to protect the virtue of their beholders; but the purple scarf that conceals their mutilated manly beauty itself a flaunting provocation.

It is the subtlety which I am afraid fools Mr. Michener, the nuance where we expect the blatancy of calendar art or Rubens. *Shibui* is the adjective that represents the life style toward which Japanese ethos aspires; and *shibui* means something between astringent and austere. To the true Zen devoté, the *shibui hito* with his cracked brown teapot and the single character by an ancient calligrapher on his wall, the impact of the *bijin* is like Marilyn Monroe. To our earlier critics, those girls of Harunobu, as supple and evasive as an erotic dream, looked like the angels of a fourteenth-century Italian fresco; and even to Mr. Michener their promise of the subtlest of frictions seems "aloof, solemn and proper." Alas!

Missoula, Montana
—1954

The Middle Against Both Ends

I AM surely one of the few people pretending to intellectual respectability who can boast that he has read more comic books than attacks on comic books. I do not mean that I have consulted or studied the comics—I have read them, often with some pleasure. Nephews and nieces, my own children, and the children of neighbors have brought them to me to share their enjoyment. An old lady on a ferry boat in Puget Sound once dropped two in my lap in wordless sympathy: I was wearing, at the time, a sailor's uniform.

I have somewhat more difficulty in getting through the books that attack them. I am put off, to begin with, by inaccuracies of fact. When Mr. Geoffrey Wagner in his *Parade of Pleasure* calls Superboy "Superman's brother" (he is, of course, Superman himself as a child), I am made suspicious. Actually, Mr. Wagner's book is one of the least painful on the subject; confused, to be sure, but quite lively and not in the least smug; though it propounds the preposterous theory that the whole of "popular literature" is a conspiracy on the part of the "plutos" to corrupt an innocent American people. Such easy melodrama can only satisfy someone prepared to believe, as Mr. Wagner apparently does, that the young girls of Harlem are being led astray by the *double-entendres* of blues records!

Mr. Wagner's notions are at least more varied and subtle than Mr. Gershon Legman's, who cries out in his *Love and Death* that it is simply our sexual frustrations which breed a popular literature dedicated to violence. But Mr. Legman's theory explains too much: not only comic books but Hemingway, war, Luce, Faulkner, the status of women—and, I should suppose, Mr. Legman's own shrill hyperboles. At that, Mr. Legman seems more to the point in his search for some deeply underlying cause than Frederic Wertham, in *Seduction of the Innocent,* with his contention that the pulps and comics in themselves are schools for murder. That the undefined aggressiveness of disturbed children can be given a shape by comic books, I do not doubt; and one could make a good case for the contention that such literature standardizes crime woefully or inhibits imagination in violence, but I find it hard to consider so obvious a symptom a prime cause of anything. Perhaps I am a little sensitive on this score, having heard the charge this week that the recent suicide of one of our college freshmen was caused by his having read (in a course of which I am in charge) Goethe, Dostoevski, and *Death of a Salesman.* Damn it, he *had* read them, and he *did* kill himself!

In none of the books on comics* I have looked into, and in none of the reports of ladies' clubs, protests of legislators, or statements of moral indignation by pastors, have I come on any real attempt to understand comic books: to define the form, midway between icon and story; to distinguish the subtypes: animal, adolescent, crime, Western, etc.; or even to separate out, from the deadpan varieties, tongue-in-cheek sports like *Pogo,* frank satire like *Mad,* or semisurrealist variations like *Plastic Man.* It would not take someone with the talents of an Aristotle, but merely with his method, to ask the rewarding questions about this kind of literature that he asked once about an equally popular and bloody genre: what are its causes and its natural form?

A cursory examination would show that the superhero comic *(Superman, Captain Marvel, Wonder Woman,* etc.) is the final form; it is statistically the most popular with the most avid readers, and it provides the only new legendary material invented along with the form rather than adapted to it.

Next, one would have to abstract the most general pattern of the myth of the superhero and deduce its significance: the urban

---

* Oddly enough, in the few years since 1955, this became a historic essay. The comic book is dead, killed, perhaps, by the tit-magazines, *Playboy,* etc.— or by T.V., on which violence has retreated to the myth from which it began, the Western.

setting, the threatened universal catastrophe, the hero who never uses arms, who returns to weakness and obscurity, who must keep his identity secret, who is impotent, etc. Not until then could one ask with any hope of an answer: what end do the comics serve? Why have they gained an immense body of readers precisely in the past fifteen or twenty years? Why must they be disguised as children's literature though read by men and women of all ages? And having answered these, one could pose the most dangerous question of all: why the constant, virulent attacks on the comics, and, indeed, on the whole of popular culture of which they are especially flagrant examples?

Strategically, if not logically, the last question should be asked first. Why the attacks? Such assaults by scientists and laymen are as characteristic of our age as puritanical diatribes against the stage of the Elizabethan Era, and pious protests against novel reading in the later eighteenth century. I suspect that a study of such conventional reactions reveals at least as much about the nature of a period as an examination of the forms to which they respond. The most fascinating and suspicious aspect of the opposition to popular narrative is its unanimity; everyone from the members of the Montana State Legislature to the ladies of the Parent Teachers Association of Boston, Massachusetts, from British M.P.'s to the wilder post-Freudians of two continents agree on this, though they may agree on nothing else. What they have in common is, I am afraid, the sense that they are all, according to their lights, righteous. And their protests represent only one more example (though an unlikely one) of the notorious failure of righteousness in matters involving art.

Just what is it with which vulgar literature is charged by various guardians of morality or sanity? With everything: encouraging crime, destroying literacy, expressing sexual frustration, unleashing sadism, spreading antidemocratic ideas, and, of course, corrupting youth. To understand the grounds of such charges, their justification and their bias, we must understand something of the nature of the subart with which we are dealing.

Perhaps it is most illuminating to begin by saying that it is a peculiarly American phenomenon, an unexpected by-product of an attempt, not only to extend literacy universally, but to delegate taste to majority suffrage. I do not mean, of course, that it is found only in the United States, but that wherever it is found, it comes first from us, and is still to be discovered in fully developed form only among us. Our experience along these lines is, in this sense, a preview for the rest of the world of what must follow the inevitable dissolution of the older aristocratic cultures.

One has only to examine certain Continental imitations of picture magazines like *Look* or *Life* or Disney-inspired cartoon books to be aware at once of the debt to American examples and of the failure of the imitations. For a true "popular literature" demands a more than ordinary slickness, the sort of high finish possible only to a machine-produced commodity in an economy of maximum prosperity. Contemporary popular culture, which is a function of an industrialized society, is distinguished from older folk art by its refusal to be shabby or second-rate in appearance, by a refusal to know its place. It is a product of the same impulse which has made available the sort of ready-made clothing which aims at destroying the possibility of knowing a lady by her dress.

Yet the articles of popular culture are made, not to be treasured, but to be thrown away; a paperback book is like a disposable diaper or a paper milk container. For all its competent finish, it cannot be preserved on dusty shelves like the calf-bound volumes of another day; indeed, its very mode of existence challenges the concept of a library, private or public. The sort of conspicuous waste once reserved for an elite is now available to anyone; and this is inconceivable without an absurdly high standard of living, just as it is unimaginable without a degree of mechanical efficiency that permits industry to replace nature, and invents—among other disposable synthetics—one for literature.

Just as the production of popular narrative demands industrial conditions most favorably developed in the United States, its distribution requires the peculiar conditions of our market places: the mass or democratized market. Subbooks and subarts are not distributed primarily through the traditional institutions: museums, libraries, and schools, which remain firmly in the hands of those who deplore mass culture. It is in drugstores and supermarkets and airline terminals that this kind of literature mingles without condescension with chocolate bars and soap flakes. We have reached the end of a long process, begun, let us say, with Samuel Richardson, in which the work of art has approached closer and closer to the status of a commodity. Even the comic book is a last descendant of *Pamela,* the final consequence of letting the tastes (or more precisely, the buying power) of a class unpledged to maintaining the traditional genres determine literary success or failure.

Those who cry out now that the work of a Mickey Spillane or *The Adventures of Superman* travesty the novel forget that the novel was long accused of travestying literature. What seems to offend us most is not the further downgrading of literary standards so much as the fact that the medium, the very notion and shape of a book, is being parodied by the comics. Jazz or the movies, which are also popular urban arts, depending for their distribution and acceptance on developments in technology (for jazz the gramophone), really upset us much less.

It is the final, though camouflaged, rejection of literacy implicit in these new forms which is the most legitimate source of distress; but all arts so universally consumed have been for illiterates, even stained glass windows and the plays of Shakespeare. What is new in our present situation, and hence especially upsetting, is that this is the first art for *post*-literates, i.e., for those who have refused the benefit for which they were presumed to have sighed in their long exclusion. Besides, modern popular narrative is disconcertingly not oral; it will not surrender the benefits of the printing press as a machine, however indifferent it may be to that press as the perpetrator of techniques devised first for pen or quill. Everything that the press can provide—except matter to be really read—is demanded: picture, typography, even in many cases the illusion of reading along with the relaxed pleasure of illiteracy. Yet the new popular forms remain somehow prose narrative or pictographic substitutes for the novel; even the cognate form of the movies is notoriously more like a novel than a play in its handling of time, space and narrative progression.

From the folk literature of the past, which ever since the triumph of the machine we have been trying sentimentally to recapture, popular literature differs in its rejection of the picturesque. Rooted in prose rather than in verse, secular rather than religious in origin, defining itself against the city rather than the world of outdoor nature, a by-product of the factory rather than agriculture, present-day popular literature defeats romantic expectations of peasants in their embroidered blouses chanting or plucking balalaikas for the approval of their betters. The haters of our own popular art love to condescend to the folk; and on records or in fashionable night clubs in recent years, we have had entertainers who have earned enviable livings producing commercial imitations of folk songs. But contemporary vulgar culture is brutal and disturbing: the quasi-spontaneous expression of the uprooted and culturally dispossessed inhabitants of anonymous cities, contriving mythologies which reduce to manageable form the threat of science, the horror of unlimited war, the general spread of corruption in a world where the social bases of old loyalties and heroisms have long been destroyed. That such an art is exploited for profit in a commercial society, mass-produced by nameless collaborators, standardized and debased, is of secondary importance. It is the patented nightmare of us all, a packaged way of coming to terms with one's environment sold for a dime to all those who have rejected the unasked-for gift of literacy.

Thought of in this light, the comic books with their legends of the eternally threatened metropolis eternally protected by immaculate and modest heroes (who shrink back after each exploit into the image of the crippled newsboy, the impotent and cowardly reporter) are seen as inheritors, for all their superficial differences, of the *inner* impulses of traditional folk art. Their gross drawing, their poverty of language, cannot disguise their heritage of aboriginal violence, their exploitation of the ancient conflict of black magic and white. Beneath their journalistic commentary on A-bomb and communism, they touch archetypal material: those shared figures of our lower minds more like the patterns of dream than fact. In a world where men threaten to dissolve into their most superficial and mechanical techniques, to become their borrowed newspaper platitudes, they remain close to the impulsive, subliminal life. They are our not quite machine-subdued Grimm, though the Black Forest has become, as it must, the City; the Wizard, the Scientist; and Simple Hans, Captain Marvel. In a society which thinks of itself as "scientific"—and of the Marvelous as childish—such a literature must seem primarily children's literature, though, of course, it is read by people of all ages.

We are now in a position to begin to answer the question: what do the righteous really have against comic books? In some parts of the world, simply the fact that they are American is sufficient, and certain homegrown self-contemners follow this line even in the United States. But it is really a minor argument, lent a certain temporary importance by passing political exigencies. To declare oneself against "the Americanization of culture" is meaningless unless one is set resolutely against industrialization and mass education.

More to the point is the attack on mass culture for its betrayal of literacy itself. In a very few cases, this charge is made seriously and with full realization of its import; but most often it amounts to nothing but an accusation of "bad grammar" or "slang" on the part of some schoolmarm to whom the spread of "different than" seems to threaten the future of civilized discourse. What should set us on guard in this case is that it is not the fully literate, the intellectuals and serious writers, who lead the attack, but the insecure semiliterate. In America, there is something a little absurd about the indignant delegation from the Parent Teachers Association (themselves clutching the latest issue of *Life*) crying out in defense of literature. Asked for suggestions, such critics are likely to propose *The Readers Digest* as required reading in high school—or to urge more comic book versions of the "classics": emasculated Melville, expurgated Hawthorne, or a child's version of something "uplifting" like "The Fall of the House of Usher." In other countries, corresponding counterparts are not hard to find.

As a matter of fact, this charge is scarcely ever urged with much conviction. It is really the portrayal of crime and horror (and less usually sex) that the enlightened censors deplore. It has been charged against vulgar art that it is sadistic, fetishistic, brutal, full of terror; that it pictures women with exaggeratedly full breasts and rumps, portrays death on the printed page, is often covertly homosexual, etc., etc. About these charges, there are two obvious things to say. First, by and large, they are true. Second, they are also true

about much of the most serious art of our time, especially that produced in America.

There is no count of sadism and brutality which could not be
equally proved against Hemingway or Faulkner or Paul Bowles—
or, for that matter, Edgar Allan Poe. There are certain more literate critics who are victims of their own confusion in this regard;
and who will condemn a Class B movie for its images of flagellation
or bloodshed only to praise in the next breath such an orgy of
high-minded sadism as *Le Salaire de la Peur*. The politics of the
French picture may be preferable, or its photography; but this cannot redeem the scene in which a mud-and-oil-soaked truck driver
crawls from a pit of sludge to reveal the protruding white bones of
the multiple fracture of the thigh. This is as much horror-pornography as *Scarface* or *Little Caesar*. You cannot condemn *Superman*
for the exploitation of violence, and praise the existentialist-homo-
sexual-sadist shockers of Paul Bowles. It is possible to murmur by
way of explanation something vague about art or catharsis; but no
one is ready to advocate the suppression of anything merely because it is aesthetically bad. In this age of conflicting standards, we
would all soon suppress each other.

An occasional Savonarola is, of course, ready to make the total
rejection; and secretly or openly, the run-of-the-mill condemner of
mass culture does condemn, on precisely the same grounds, most
contemporary literature of distinction. Historically, one can make
quite a convincing case to prove that our highest and lowest arts
come from a common antibourgeois source. Edgar Allan Poe, who
lived the image of the Dandy that has been haunting high art ever
since, also, one remembers, invented the popular detective story;
and there is a direct line from Hemingway to O'Hara to Dashiell
Hammett to Raymond Chandler to Mickey Spillane to Richard S.
Prather.

Of both lines of descent from Poe, one can say that they tell a
black and distressing truth (we are creatures of dark impulse in a
threatened and guilty world), and that they challenge the more genteel versions of "good taste." Behind the opposition to vulgar literature, there is at work the same fear of the archetypal and the unconscious itself that motivated similar attacks on Elizabethan
drama and on the eighteenth-century novel. We always judge Gos-

son a fool in terms of Shakespeare; but this is not the point—he was just as wrong in his attack on the worst written, the most outrageously bloody and bawdy plays of his time. I should hate my argument to be understood as a defense of what is banal and mechanical and dull (there is, of course, a great deal!) in mass culture; it is merely a counterattack against those who are aiming through that banality and dullness at what moves all literature of worth. Anyone at all sensitive to the life of the imagination would surely prefer his kids to read the coarsest fables of Black and White contending for the City of Man, rather than have them spell out, "Oh, see, Jane. Funny, funny Jane," or read to themselves hygienic accounts of the operation of supermarkets or manureless farms. Yet most schoolboard members are on the side of mental hygiene; and it is they who lead the charge against mass culture.

Anyone old enough to have seen, say, *Rain* is on guard against those who in the guise of wanting to destroy savagery and ignorance wage war on spontaneity and richness. But we are likely to think of such possibilities purely in sexual terms; the new righteous themselves have been touched lightly by Freud and are firm believers in frankness and "sex education." But in the midst of their self-congratulation at their emancipation, they have become victims of a new and ferocious prudery. One who would be ashamed to lecture his masturbating son on the dangers of insanity, is quite prepared (especially if he has been reading Wertham) to predict the electric chair for the young scoundrel with a bootlegged comic. Superman is our Sadie Thompson. We live in an age when the child who is exposed to the "facts of life" is protected from "the facts of death." In the United States, for instance, a certain Doctor Spock has produced an enlightened guide to child care for modern mothers—a paperback book which sold, I would guess, millions of copies. Tell the child all about sex, the good doctor advises, but on the subject of death—hush!

By more "advanced" consultants, the taboo is advanced further toward absurdity: no blood-soaked Grimm, no terrifying Andersen, no childhood verses about cradles that fall—for fear breeds insecurity; insecurity, aggression; aggression, war. There is even a "happy," that is to say, expurgated, Mother Goose in which the three blind mice have become "kind mice"—and the farmer's wife no longer hacks off their tails, but "cuts them some cheese with a carving knife." Everywhere the fear of fear is endemic, the fear of the very names of fear; those who have most ardently desired to end warfare and personal cruelty in the world around them, and are therefore most frustrated by their persistence, conspire to stamp out violence on the nursery bookshelf. This much they can do anyhow. If they can't hold up the weather, at least they can break the bloody glass.

This same fear of the instinctual and the dark, this denial of death and guilt by the enlightened genteel, motivates their distrust of serious literature, too. Faulkner is snubbed and the comic books are banned, not in the interests of the classics or even of Robert Louis Stevenson, as the attackers claim, but in the name of a literature of the middle ground which finds its fictitious vision of a kindly and congenial world attacked from above and below. I speak now not of the few intellectual converts to the cause of censorship, but of the main body of genteel book-banners, whose idol is Lloyd Douglas or even A. J. Cronin. When a critic like Mr. Wagner is led to applaud what he sees as a "trend" toward making doctors, lawyers, etc. the heroes of certain magazine stories, he has fallen into the trap of regarding middling fiction as a transmission belt from the vulgar to the high. There is no question, however, of a slow climb from the level of literature which celebrates newspaper reporters, newsboys, radio commentators (who are also superheroes in tight-fitting uniforms with insignia), through one which centers around prosperous professionals, to the heights of serious literature, whose protagonists are suicides full of incestuous longings, lady lushes with clipped hair, bootleggers, gangsters, and broken-down pugs. To try to state the progression is to reveal its absurdity.

The conception of such a "trend" is nothing more than the standard attitude of a standard kind of literature, the literature of slick-paper ladies' magazines, which prefers the stereotype to the archetype, loves poetic justice, sentimentality, and gentility, and is peopled by characters who bathe frequently, live in the suburbs, and are professionals. Such literature circles mindlessly inside the trap of its two themes: unconsummated adultery and the consummated pure romance. There can be little doubt about which kind of

persons and which sort of fables best typify our plight, which tell
the truth—or better: a truth in the language of those to whom they
speak.

In the last phrase, there is a rub. The notion that there is more
than one language of art, or rather, that there is something not
quite art, which performs art's function for most men in our society, is disquieting enough for anyone, and completely unaccepta-
ble to the sentimental egalitarian, who had dreamed of universal literacy leading directly to a universal culture. It is here that we begin
to see that there is a politics as well as a pathology involved in the
bourgeois hostility to popular culture. I do not refer only to the explicit political ideas embodied in the comics or in the literature of
the cultural élite; but certainly each of these arts has a characteristic attitude: populist-authoritarian on the one hand, and aristocratic-
authoritarian on the other.

It is notorious how few of the eminent novelists or poets of our
time have shared the political ideals we (most readers of this magazine and I) would agree are the most noble available to us. The flir-
tations of Yeats and Lawrence with fascism, Pound's weird amal-
gam of Confucianism, Jeffersonianism, and Social Credit, the
modified Dixiecrat principles of Faulkner—all make the point with
terrible reiteration. Between the best art and poetry of our age and
the critical liberal reader there can be no bond of shared belief; at
best we have the ironic confrontation of the skeptical mind and the
believing imagination. It is this division which has, I suppose, led us
to define more and more narrowly the "aesthetic experience," to attempt to isolate a quality of seeing and saying that has a moral
value quite independent of *what* is seen or heard.

> Time that with this strange excuse
> Pardoned Kipling and his views,
> And will pardon Paul Claudel,
> Pardons him for writing well.

But the genteel middling mind which turns to art for entertainment and uplift, finds this point of view reprehensible, and cries out
in rage against those who give Ezra Pound a prize and who claim
that "to permit other considerations than that of poetic achievement

to sway the decision world . . . deny the validity of that objective perception of value on which any civilized society must rest." We live in the midst of a strange two-front class war: the readers of the slicks battling the subscribers to the "little reviews" and the consumers of pulps; the sentimental-egalitarian conscience against the ironical-aristocratic sensibility on the one hand and the brutal-populist mentality on the other. The joke, of course, is that it is the "democratic" center which calls here and now for suppression of its rivals; while the elite advocate a condescending tolerance, and the vulgar ask only to be let alone.

It is disconcerting to find cultural repression flourishing at the point where middling culture meets a kindly, if not vigorously thought-out, liberalism. The sort of right-thinking citizen who subsidizes trips to America for Japanese girls scarred by the Hiroshima bombing and deplores McCarthy in the public press also deplores, and would censor, the comics. In one sense, this is fair enough; for beneath the veneer of slogans that "crime doesn't pay" and the superficial praise of law and order, the comics do reflect that dark populist faith which Senator McCarthy has exploited. There is a kind of "black socialism" of the American masses which underlies formal allegiances to one party or another: the sense that there is always a conspiracy at the centers of political and financial power; the notion that the official defenders of the commonwealth are "bought" more often than not; an impatience with moral scruples and a distrust of intelligence, especially in the expert and scientist; a willingness to identify the enemy, the dark projection of everything most feared in the self, with some journalistically-defined political opponent of the moment.

This is not quite the "fascism" it is sometimes called. There is, for instance, no European anti-Semitism involved, despite the conventional hooked nose of the scientist-villain. (The inventors and chief producers of comic books have been, as it happens, Jews.) There is also no adulation of a dictator figure on the model of Hitler or Stalin; though one of the archetypes of the Deliverer in the comics is called Superman, he is quite unlike the Nietzschean figure —it is the image of Cincinnatus which persists in him, an archetype that has possessed the American imagination since the time of Washington: the leader who enlists for the duration and retires unrewarded to obscurity.

It would be absurd to ask the consumer of such art to admire in the place of images that project his own impotence and longing for civil peace some hero of middling culture—say, the good boy of Arthur Miller's *Death of a Salesman,* who, because he has studied hard in school, has become a lawyer who argues cases before the Supreme Court and has friends who own their own tennis courts. As absurd as to ask the general populace to worship Stephen Dedalus or Captain Ahab! But the high-minded petty-bourgeois cannot understand or forgive the rejection of his own dream, which he considers as nothing less than the final dream of humanity. The very existence of a kind of art based on allegiances and values other than his challenges an article of his political faith; and when such an art is "popular," that is, more read, more liked, more bought than his own, he feels his *raison d'être,* his basic life defense, imperiled. The failure of the petty bourgeoisie to achieve cultural hegemony threatens their dream of a truly classless society; for they believe, with some justification, that such a society can afford only a single culture. And they see, in the persistence of a high art and a low art on either side of their average own, symptoms of the re-emergence of classes in a quarter where no one had troubled to stand guard.

The problem posed by popular culture is finally, then, a problem of class distinction in a democratic society. What is at stake is the refusal of cultural equality by a large part of the population. It is misleading to think of popular culture as the product of a conspiracy of profiteers against the rest of us. This venerable notion of an eternally oppressed and deprived but innocent people is precisely what the rise of mass culture challenges. Much of what upper-class egalitarians dreamed for him, the ordinary man does not want—especially literacy. The situation is bewildering and complex, for the people have not rejected completely the notion of cultural equality; rather, they desire its symbol but not its fact. At the very moment when half of the population of the United States reads no *hardcover* book in a year, more than half of all high school graduates are entering universities and colleges; in twenty-five years almost all Americans will at least begin a higher education. It is clear that what is demanded is a B.A. for everyone, with the stipulation that no one be forced to read to get it. And this the colleges, with "objective tests" and "visual aids," are doing their reluctant best to satisfy.

One of the more exasperating aspects of the cultural defeat of the egalitarians is that it followed a seeming victory. For a while (in the Anglo-Saxon world at least) it appeared as if the spread of literacy, the rise of the bourgeoisie, and the emergence of the novel as a reigning form would succeed in destroying both traditional folk art and an aristocratic literature still pledged to epic, ode, and verse tragedy. But the novel itself (in the hands of Lawrence, Proust, Kafka, etc.) soon passed beyond the comprehension of those for whom it was originally contrived; and the retrograde derivations from it—various steps in a retreat toward wordless narrative: digests, pulp fiction, movies, picture magazines—revealed that middling literature was not in fact the legitimate heir of either folk art or high art, much less the successor of both, but a *tertium quid* of uncertain status and value.

The middlebrow reacts with equal fury to an art that baffles his understanding and to one which refuses to aspire to his level. The first reminds him that he has not yet, after all, *arrived* (and, indeed, may never make it); the second suggests to him a condition to which he might easily relapse, one perhaps that might have made him happier with less effort (and here exacerbated puritanism is joined to baffled egalitarianism)—even suggests what his state may appear like to those a notch above. Since he cannot on his own terms explain to himself why anyone should choose any level but the highest (that is, his own), the failure of the vulgar seems to him the product of mere ignorance and laziness—a crime! And the rejection by the advanced artist of his canons strikes him as a finicking excess, a pointless and unforgivable snobbism. Both, that is, suggest the intolerable notion of a hierarchy of taste, a hierarchy of values, the possibility of cultural classes in a democratic state; and before this, puzzled and enraged, he can only call a cop. The fear of the vulgar is the obverse of the fear of excellence, and both are aspects of the fear of difference: symptoms of a drive for conformity on the level of the timid, sentimental, mindless-bodiless genteel.

—1955

What Shining Phantom:
Writers and the Movies

IN *The Boys in the Back Room,* a little book first published in 1941 (which is to say, at the end of the decade during which serious writers first went in large numbers to Hollywood), Edmund Wilson turns uncustomarily to verse—perhaps because for once he is moved too deeply for prose. *What shining phantom,* he asks, *folds its wings before us?/ What apparition, smiling yet remote?/ Is this—so portly yet so lightly porous—/ The old friend who went west and never wrote?* And toward the end of that same book, reflecting on the then recent deaths of F. Scott Fitzgerald and Nathanael West, both friends like the anonymous nonwriter in his poem, Wilson turns to prose to make explicit his intent. "Both West and Fitzgerald," he explains, "were writers of a conscience and with natural gifts rare enough in America or anywhere; and their failure to get the best out of their years may certainly be laid partly to Hollywood, with its already appalling record of talent depraved and wasted."

In prose or verse, however, what Mr. Wilson provides us is more poetry than truth, a conventional elegy rather than a series of insights, as might well be expected from a critic whose range of understanding did not extend to the world of pop culture in general, or that of the "pratfall," the "weenie," the "gag," and the "big take" (movie jargon which Mr. Wilson uses with all the unconvincingness of Walt Whitman turning on his French) in particular. What was involved in the flight of writers to Hollywood and their inevitable defeat there was not so much a series of betrayals and appropriate punishments, as the first stage in a revolution—only recently defined by such commentators as Marshall McLuhan—which would make print obsolete and the first panicked attempts of those committed to the old regime of words to come to terms with the future.

Yet once upon a time Mr. Wilson's fable (only lately reprinted without the prefatory verses in *Classics and Commercials)* was taken as literal fact; and it remains, in certain nostalgic quarters—especially where reinforced by vestiges of thirties-type liberalism—a staple of pretentious journalism. Malcolm Cowley, for instance, writing in 1966 about William Faulkner (whose example should have taught him better), submits to the old routine: ". . . Hollywood, which used to have a notorious fashion of embracing and destroying men of letters," he starts in an offhand way; and continues, "After publishing an admired book, or two or three, the writer was offered a contract by a movie studio; then he bought a house with a swimming pool and vanished from print. If he reappeared years later, it was usually with a novel designed to have the deceptive appeal of an uplift brassiere."

Perhaps it was necessary not only to have sold oneself to the movies but also to have bought a swimming pool to make it into Mr. Cowley's category of the damned; for surely the post-Hollywood novels of both Fitzgerald and West, *The Last Tycoon* and *The Day of the Locust,* have an appeal based on something more substantial than foam rubber. More specious than either, to be sure, are the Pat Hobby short stories of Fitzgerald, purely commercial ventures in which Fitzgerald travestied and stereotyped his own situation as an unsuccessful writer of scripts; and among the clichés deployed in these seventeen or more attempts at pandering to popular notions of life in Hollywood is Pat's memory of the magnificent swimming pool he possessed in his time of glory. ". . . When Pat had his pool in those fat days of silent pictures," Fitzgerald tells us in "A Patriotic Short," "it was entirely cement, unless you should count the cracks where the water stubbornly sought its own level through the mud."

West, too, however—in work considerably above the level of potboiling—is obsessed by the banal image (a motion picture image, really, its ironies obvious enough for the obtusest audience), taking time out from the grimmer concerns of *The Day of the Locust* to let us know that Claude Estee—the single successful screen writer in the book—has the required pool with its required significances. But West, of course, redeems this cliché in the same surreal fashion he redeems so many others, by putting a dead horse (a *fake* dead horse, naturally) at the bottom of the pool. Yet even a dead horse does not help for long—disappearing for instance, from the pool in Evelyn Waugh's *The Loved One,* to make possible once more the pristine Wilsonian sentimentality. In the course of describing the house of Sir Francis Hinsley (formerly "the only knight in Hollywood" and "chief script-writer in Megalopolitan Pictures"), Waugh lingers over his now abandoned swimming pool, which, he informs us, "had once flashed like an aquarium with the limbs of long-departed beauties" before it had become "cracked and over-grown with weeds." All of which was quite literally reproduced on the screen—where it belonged to begin with—in the recent film version of Waugh's novel.

Well, swimming pools have ceased, even mythologically, to represent Hollywood, not because any banality ever wears out on its own; but because prosperity has brought that legendary pleasure from dreamland to the backyards of suburbia, and—in what survives of its former legendary glory—to that storehouse of the dreams of the thirties, Hugh Heffner's pleasure palace in Chicago. The suburban swimming pool is memorialized in a story by John Cheever called "The Swimmer," which recounts the dream legend of a commuter who swam all the way home from the station through pool after pool after pool of his neighbors; and even now that story is—of course, of course—in the process of becoming a movie.

Yet the legend survives its trappings; the myth of "the old friend who went west" outlives the Hollywood swimming pool. Some such "old friends" at least are still wincing, perhaps protesting too much: Daniel Fuchs, for instance, who comes closest to having lived the mythological history of Wilson's "shining phantom." Fuchs had written three novels before going off to Hollywood toward the end of the thirties, *Summer in Williamsburg,* *Homage to Blenholt,* and *Low Company,* none of which were much "admired" (the word is his) when they appeared. "The books didn't sell—400 copies, 400, 1200," Fuchs himself reports. "The reviews were scanty, immaterial." And so, he went to Hollywood, made it there, lived long enough to see his reputation revived, his novels reprinted in the sixties—but remained bugged all the time, it would appear, by the judgment implicit in Wilson's vision. At any rate, he uses the occasion of the re-issue of his fiction in a single volume in 1961 to go on record: "The popular notions about the movies aren't true. It takes a good deal of energy and hard sense to write stories over an extended period of time, and it would be foolish to expect writers not to want to be paid a livelihood for what they do. But we are engaged here on the same problems that perplex writers everywhere. We grapple with the daily mystery. We struggle with form, with Chimera . . . 'Poesy,' my father used to call it, and I know I will keep at it as long as I can, because surely there is nothing else to do."

It would be easier to believe Fuchs if he seemed really to believe himself; but he is as much of a child of his age and Wilson's, of those mythicized and mythicizing thirties, as was James M. Cain, who had already cried out against Wilson twenty years before—and with more apparent cause, being one of the "boys in the backroom" specifically attacked by Wilson. "Edmund Wilson. . . in an article he wrote about me . . .," James M. Cain complained in 1942 in a preface to three of his own novelettes, "attributed these socko twists and surprises to a leaning toward Hollywood, which is not particularly the case." And he goes on to explain that, despite the tutoring of a script writer called Vincent Lawrence, he himself just "couldn't write pictures," which he takes to be some guarantee, we gather, of virtue as well as of ineptitude. But we remember that, though Mr. Cain may have written no successful scripts, he was the author of "Double Indemnity," as well as of *The Postman Always Rings Twice,*" which is to say, of certain not very good books which *became* very good films—the sort of transitional figure between a Gutenberg era and a non-Gutenberg one (the late Hemingway would be another example, and Steinbeck most of the time), whom we have not understood very well until now: the author of embryo movies which only pretend to be books. Cain, indeed, must be given double credit; since he not only provided the cue for several first-rate American screenplays, but the inspiration as well for Visconti's *Ossessione* (born of an encounter between *The Postman Always Rings Twice* and the Italian director's characteristic blend of social protest and High Camp), with which "neorealism" was born.

All this, however, has to do not with being "depraved and wasted" in any conventional sense but with being fulfilled and completed in a quite unforeseen way. No, the notion of being "depraved and wasted," or, alternatively, "embraced and destroyed" belongs to the legendary literature of defunct "modernism"—to what we can readily see now is the realm of myth rather than that of history or sociology. It is a special development, which flourished chiefly in the thirties, of that Cult of Self-Pity which underlies much of the literature of the first half of the twentieth century. The notion of society as a conspiracy against the individual, and of art as a protest against that conspiracy goes back as far as the beginnings of Romanticism at least. Originally, however, the artist himself was not thought of as the sole or exclusive victim of the world, women and children and noble savages, even peasants and workers being quite understandably preferred.

After World War I, however, writers in Anglo-Saxon countries (responding belatedly to cues from the French) began to portray the poet himself as the victim *par excellence* and to shop about for the institutions most inimical to his career. To such basically European writers as James Joyce, for instance, the traditional institutions of Christendom seemed quite satisfactory: the Family, the Church, the State; but these have struck latterday Americans as somehow outdated compared with the newer institutions (the threat of the future rather than the encumbrance of the past) of mass culture, including mass war. But the notion of total war as particularly reprehensible because of the masterpieces it inhibits or destroys (a notion pathetically developed in, say, Dos Passos's *Three Soldiers)* seems finally a little absurd. And, in any case, our writers have chosen to think of themselves as being destroyed—more ironically than pathetically—by advanced technological substitutes for their own discipline: advertising, script writing, publish-or-perish scholarship, television.

Besides, most men, even writers, are *drafted* into wars—raped as it were, whereas, they are *tempted* into other areas of mass culture, seduced or prostituted. In Peter Viertel's *White Hunter, Black*

Heart, which appeared late enough (1953) to seem a retrospective catalogue of all the anti-Hollywood clichés, a semifictional character, transparently modeled on John Huston, is permitted to comment at length on this metaphor, crying out, "They mean the whores when they say Hollywood. . . . Now get this, Victor . . . whores have to sell one of the few things that shouldn't be for sale in this world: love. But there are other things that shouldn't be for sale beside love, you know. . . . There are the whores who sell words and ideas and melodies. . . . Now I know what I'm talking about . . . because I've hustled a little in my time, a hell of a lot more than I like to admit I have. . . . Well, anyway, my point is that it's the whores who put up Hollywood as a big target, and very often they shoot at it themselves just to feel clean again. . . ." Once more we find ourselves in that dim area of protest and apologetics in which muddled voices cry, "You're one, too!" or "I may be one, but not full time," or, "not as much as you."

Money and guilt and the denial of guilt: these are, at any rate, key terms in all accounts of Hollywood; though for a long time, as a matter of fact, not "selling oneself" but "selling out" (another one of those slightly alien terms imported by Marxists into American life during the thirties), an image more sociological than erotic, possessed the minds of those who sought to make fiction of an experience already fictional in essence. The anti-Hollywood Novel— that writer's ultimate, even sometimes posthumous revenge on his seducer-employers—is basically a Depression product; for the heyday of the in-and-out writer in Hollywood, the classic period memorialized in the classic books, coincides almost exactly with that somewhat more than a decade we call the thirties.

The thirties as a social-psychological phenomenon begins with the stock-market crash of late 1927 or, perhaps, with the execution of Sacco and Vanzetti earlier in that same year, and ends with the Japanese attack on Pearl Harbor on December 7, 1941; while the legendary era for the writer in Hollywood begins with the perfection of "talking pictures" in 1927—with Al Jolson in *The Jazz Singer,* let's say, making it on the screen by singing the death of two worlds: the Minstrel Show and Orthodox Judaism—and ends with a corresponding double death, the demise within a few days of each other, during December 1940, of Scott Fitzgerald and Nathanael West. The novels which comment on that era reflect inevitably, then, its fashionable class consciousness; but since the experience which produced them had to come first, they do not begin to appear until that class consciousness, at first vulgar and surly and truly embattled, had become attenuated and sentimental and token.

They are a subvariety not of the Proletarian Novel proper, which belongs to pre-1935, the time of Mike Gold and Grace Lumpkin and Jack Conroy, but of the Popular Front Novel, like *Grapes of Wrath,* for instance, which arises out of a world conditioned by the rhetoric of such Hollywood politicos as Donald Ogden Stewart, and which disappears back into the clichés of that world without a struggle. In the declining thirties, as a matter of fact, when writers of real eminence were deserting the ranks of the communist fellow travelers, hack script writers were replacing them in the leadership of movements like the League Against War and Fascism; and the old vision of the high-paid Hollywood professional as necessarily a whore and sellout had to be qualified.

A division began to be made, in popular mythology and fiction alike, between the kind of successful screen writer who joins the Screen Writers Guild and/or tries to smuggle favorable references to Loyalist Spain and the Soviet Union into his scripts, and the kind who refuses to pay dues in the workers' cause and/or give lip service to "Humanity" as defined by the Communist Party. In the encoded cant of the time, the former, being only half-whores or not-quite-whores, were referred to as the "decent and progressive forces"; and it came to be believed that "decent and progressive" novelists, desiring to treat justly the environment which bred them, ought to populate their novels with a preponderance of such types. Woe unto those who did not! Even poor Budd Schulberg, who in his best-selling *What Makes Sammy Run* had rewarded his Jewish narrator-hero ("a decent, generous and gifted" screen writer and Guild member) with the hand of an Anglo-Saxon heroine (an even more "decent, generous, and gifted" screen writer and Guild member), was abused for having insisted too much on the villainy and success of the Jewish heel who gives his book its name.

But he made amends by carrying over into his second book about the movies, *The Disenchanted,* a minor "decent, gifted, etc."

character from the first, a certain Julian Blumberg, whom he permits to be kind to a sodden, aging, unsuccessful screen writer, obviously intended to represent Scott Fitzgerald; and appears himself, faintly disguised, to lecture the same failing lush on the virtues of "progressivism." It is all a little disheartening, but fair enough, I suppose, in light of the fact that Fitzgerald had in fact flirted with left-wing politics, perhaps under the influence of Donald Ogden Stewart, with whom he had worked on a script; and had paid his respects to that flirtation in the embarrassingly bad scene in *The Last Tycoon* which describes a fist fight between the brilliant but failing Jewish producer, Monroe Stahr, and a (Jewish?) communist organizer called Brimmer ("a little on the order of Spencer Tracy. . ." poor Fitzgerald describes him). At the close of the scene, the producer lies on the floor, cold-cocked with a single symbolic punch; and to make the allegorical meanings of the encounter clear, Fitzgerald has his girl narrator, partly responsible for the conflict and a witness throughout, comment about Brimmer, ". . . afterward I thought it looked as if he were saying, "Is *this* all? This frail half-sick person holding up the whole thing?"

Only Nathanael West managed to resist the temptation to redeem the Hollywood writer by reminding us that he was tithing himself for Spain or meeting secretly with others of his kind to condemn the system by which he lived; and even West felt obliged to apologize privately, in a letter to the now almost forgotten Proletarian Novelist Jack Conroy: "If I put into *The Day of the Locust* any of the sincere, honest people who work here and are making such a great, progressive fight. . . the whole fabric of the peculiar half-world which I attempted to create would be badly torn by them." In the letter itself, we watch his rhetoric go fashionably soft and realize that only his exclusion of those whom the age (with West assenting) conspired to think virtuous kept his novel as bleak and antisentimental as it had to be for truth's sake.

When the "progressive" self-deception of the Popular Front had given way to the "anticommunist" self-righteousness of the McCarthy era, the "sincere, honest people" who had persuaded themselves that somehow they were *really* boring from within, even as they made it big in Hollywood, were disconcertingly taken at their word by Congressional Investigating Committees; and they had, therefore, to choose between public recantation and informing, on the one hand, or silence and exile, on the other, exile from the industry that had for so long permitted them both swimming pools *and* clean consciences. There have been two major attempts at dealing with those who made the choice, one way or the other: the first by Norman Mailer, who deals with a recanter; and the other by Mordecai Richler, who treats those who stood firm and were exiled; and oddly enough (though perhaps not unexpectedly) the recanters come off a little better than the unreconstructed.

Mailer's *The Deer Park* begins as the outsider's dream (nurtured in part by other earlier books) of Hollywood people disporting themselves at Palm Springs, and ends as a sympathetic study of the vain and gifted director, an almost hero, who gives up his lifelong resistance to the world in which he flourishes, when he learns first to love, then to be defeated and die. Richler, on the other hand, begins completely outside of Hollywood and its environs, portraying in *Choice of Enemies* the life in England (where Richler himself, a Canadian by birth, is a screen writer) of certain left-wing refugees from Hollywood, who still try to play, without power and on immensely diminished funds, the old games of backbiting and ass-kissing and self-congratulation and betrayal. Both Mailer's book and Richler's, however, though obviously the products of talented younger writers, seemed even at the moment of their appearance, imitations or refinements of a mode still viable, perhaps, but no longer mythically potent.

By 1955, surely, when *The Deer Park* was published, we needed no Sergius O'Shaughnessy come back from the grave to tell us the truth about Southern California and the movies; for the truth had been invented before the fact and, whatever its effectiveness once, had long since ceased to move anyone but actors. How much more remote and unconvincing, then, that same world of Mailer's seemed in 1967, when, after long long delays, the play he had been making of his novel all those years finally got onto the stage, where (with true lack of discretion) it is being presented right now, not as a period piece but as something current or, at least, timeless. Such trifling with time is necessary, I suppose, if *The Deer Park* is eventually to be made into a movie, since the men who make movies cannot really confess that they are dead, that all their writers are ghost writers, their players ghost players, and even the producers ghosts like the rest. And *The Deer Park must* be made into a movie so that we can all be quit of a legend we seem to have known forever, without that knowledge having ever done any of us a bit of good.

Certainly it did not help Mailer, who—knowing what he must have known, what his book reveals he knew—went anyhow to Hollywood. But why, we ask, *why?* And not only of Mailer; since delusion was built into Hollywood from the start, and no one ever went there without his eyes open. Into wars, writers may have carried for a little while illusions to be lost; and similarly the universities once dangled before them fair promises and enticing hopes, as did even the Revolutionary Movement of the Depression years and the Popular Front Days which followed. But what ever drew writers to Hollywood?

The search for destruction, I am tempted to answer off the cuff, a desire to play Russian roulette, if not to die—to act out in their own particular lives the fate of the literary art to which they have committed themselves, the fate of books in the world of Hollywood, whose normal temperature is Fahrenheit 451 (the temperature at which as everyone now knows—since Ray Bradbury's book of that name has been consumed in a film, too—all paper burns). But perhaps it is much simpler than that—they go just to make money, as Wilson suggested, or to find a subject for a book, as all the rebuttals to him have really answered, whatever they pretended to say. Or maybe after all, it is a mythological journey, in the full sense of the word, as a descent into all that Hell used to be; for surely "Hollywood" is just as polysemous and attractively sinister a word as any of the traditional names for the underworld; though like hell itself, it has become a cliché.

Let us try once more, then, to penetrate the cliché, by turning once more to Peter Viertel's handbook of banality, to *White Hunter, Black Heart* at the place where his producer-director-villain continues to cry out in protest against platitudes: "You see, the way Vic uses the word 'Hollywood' is an insult. Now, don't contradict me. I've heard it before. In the Army, in the theater in New York —hell, everywhere. People say 'Hollywood' when they want to insult you. But it isn't an insult, really. . .Hollywood is a place where they make a product; it's the name of a factory town, just like Detroit, or Birmingham, or Schaffhausen. But because the cheap element in that town has been overadvertised, it is insulting to remind a man that he comes from there. . . but it doesn't bother me so much when they say it, because I know they're talking about the hustlers, and the flesh peddlers, and the pimps who sit in the sun out there, around the swimming pools. . . . They're not talking about the guys who work out there, who try to do something worth-while. They mean the whores. . . ."

But this takes us right back to where we started, indicating that the longest way around is the only way home (or to hell, if you please), that the swimming pools and the whores are not incidental but essential to Hollywood, which, if it is, indeed, "a factory town," is quite unlike others in that it produces not machines but men and women, living meat for use and pleasure, though (by the canny use of machines) it manages to produce them twice over—once in what *they* take for actuality, i.e., life itself, and once on what *we* take for actuality, i.e., the screen. That these men and women, this living meat be "hustlers, flesh peddlers and pimps," is precisely necessary; since Hollywood is, on the first mythological level, Sodom, or—to use Mailer's alternative title—"the Deer Park": "that gorge of innocence and virtue, in which were engulfed so many victims who when they returned to society brought with them depravity, debauchery, and all the vices they naturally acquired from the infamous officials of such a place. . . . Indeed who can reckon the expense of that band of pimps and madames. . . ." Now that the hand-held camera and a kind of ultimate vertical social mobility has placed the journey to hell within the reach of everyone, and we need no Deer Parks, no Sodom, no Hollywood—we can consider with detachment the special sexual function Hollywood once fulfilled.

It was the place (in a world which had lost the secret pleasure palaces of the aristocrats as locuses for fantasy, and which had not yet learned fully to democratize sexual reverie as well as sexual fact) which simultaneously created—and fulfilled by proxy—the wet dreams of everyone. No wonder that there is scarcely a book which uses Hollywood for a setting that does not include scenes in a whorehouse, or encounters with a pimp, or descriptions of private showings of dirty films for the makers of public films (the movies within the movie world—at least according to the anti-Hollywood novelists—were explicitly, banally pornographic, i.e., totally unclothed). But the special fable which haunts the writers of books about the bookless world of Hollywood is the actual pursuit and possession of a female star, one of those standardized erotic objects nightly possessed in fantasy by millions—superwhores, as it were, in possessing whom in fact one joins himself in fantasy with all the other males of his world, potent or demipotent or without even the power to dream unaided.

Sometimes, to be sure, we are presented, in the fictions made of the Hollywood experience, with the caricature of this sexual encounter, as the hero embraces or, better still, fails to embrace not some recognized and celebrated actress but the frantic anonymous slut aspiring to the role of the Love Goddess. In Mailer's *The Deer Park,* however, or in Fitzgerald's short story "Crazy Sunday" (his first attempt to come to terms in print with Irving Thalberg and the alluring image of Norma Shearer who was his wife) we are given fantasy triumphing over frustration: the universally desired women privately (if only momentarily) possessed. This is the place where the fiction about Hollywood aspires to poetry rather than revenge —or rather, perhaps, where the poetry of celebration and the prose of revenge improbably approach each other, two opposed traditions becoming one. Ever since films became a part of our common culture, poets—who, unlike novelists, have gone not to Hollywood with the chosen few, but just to the movies with the unnumbered many—have been singing the charms of the not-quite-unreal ladies who move through those films: from Vachel Lindsay's coyly gallant "Mae Marsh, Motion Picture Actress" ("She is a madonna in an art/ As wild and young as her sweet eyes:/ A cool dew flower from this hot lamp/ That is today's divine surprise") to Joel Oppenheimer's considerably franker "Dear Miss Monroe" (" . . . some nights i think, while/ i/m in bed, of how lovely your/ body must be, and i don/t mean of/ when the king/s hand is sneaking/ under the sheets while you two/ kiss, i mean of when you and i/ would kiss. . ."). Closer to the poems than to Fitzgerald or Mailer's evocations in prose of bitch goddesses without minds are those transformations of Marilyn *(last,* it now becomes clear, of her once apparently inexhaustible line) at the end of Mailer's own later *An*

American Dream or the first pages of Leonard Cohen's post-Hollywood novel, *Beautiful Losers.*

And somewhere on the other side of both poems and novels, behind the screen, as it were, where neither form of literature had reached before, is the strange saga of the Writer and the Star that Arthur Miller lived-wrote by first marrying Marilyn Monroe; then casting her as the anonymous aspirant to all she actually was in *The Misfits* (where she insisted all the same on being only what the screen had composed, not what Miller thought he had rewritten, loving a tree, subduing Clark Gable); then when she was dead, playing her story—the story Hollywood and the myth had determined for her—on the stage, even printing it, as if he had made it up out of the whole cloth, and were waiting for the Hollywood that no longer existed to find another starlet to play it, another John Huston to direct it, another Arthur Miller to be given the job of writing the script: as if the whole thing could continue to go round and round, as if the exact point of it all were not that it was finished, done with. *Basta.*

But what fun and games we have had before it was finished; and how our authors large and small have responded, running the whole gamut of the ambivalence proper to our culture: from nauseated horror (as in Faulkner's single, queasy story out of his Hollywood experience, "Golden Land," in which the drunken and eminently successful father of a faggot and a whore wakes to find his daughter's photograph under the headlines, APRIL LALEAR BARES ORGY SECRETS) to the kind of wistful longing, the dumb hope that rises in the heart of Mailer's dumb hero in *The Deer Park,* when a cynical producer, urging him to turn actor, cries, "You think you're going to enjoy goosing waitresses when you've been boffing the best? Brother, I can tell you, once you've been bed-wise with high-class pussy, it makes you ill, it makes you physically ill to take less than the best. . . ."

It is Nathanael West, however, who preserved the flavor and balance of the ambivalence most perfectly—in the yearning of the studio artist Tod Hackett (nearest thing to a self-portrait of West in *The Day of the Locust)* for Faye Greener, the girl who will never be a star but who embodies the erotic allure of the film heroine all the more convincingly: available to anyone with the going price of tail or with the face and body of a movie actor—but unobtainable by that very token to the only one capable of imagining her, that is, to the poor artist. A luscious seventeen-year-old in the dress of a twelve-year-old child, she flashes across the screen, her long legs "like swords" suggesting to Tod destruction and death; while behind her run (in the painting Tod dreams, at least, which only can give meaning to her life) the book's other major grotesques: a lustful dwarf, a parody cowboy, a troupe of Eskimo acrobats; and behind them, a howling crowd of witnesses—caricatures of the passive and resentful audience—enter at last upon the violence which they have too long only dreamed. The title of Tod's picture is "The Burning of Los Angeles," but the destruction of the city is only the public fantasy which masks his private dream-wish: to rape and destroy that green and golden girl (always golder and "greener" on the other side of the invisible, unpassable fence between audience and screen image), or better yet to be destroyed by her: "Her invitation wasn't to pleasure, but to struggle, hard and sharp, closer to murder than to love. If you threw yourself on her, it would be like throwing yourself from the parapet of a skyscraper. You would do it with a scream. You couldn't expect to rise again. Your teeth would be driven into your skull like nails into a pine board and your back would be broken. . . ."

It is such a love in such a setting that the writer has sought in Hollywood, or so at least West would have us believe, so he shrilly insists in the pages of the best book anyone has ever written about that oddest of "factory towns." In his vision, the metaphorical whore, who calls himself an artist ("When the Hollywood job had come along, he had grabbed it despite the arguments of his friends who were certain that he was selling out. . ."), grapples with the actual one, who calls herself an actress (" 'She's a whore!' he heard Homer grunt. . . ."), even as Sodom turns to ash, and the doomed avengers of all they have themselves desired and loved and despised riot in the streets: ". . . a great united front of screwballs and screwboxes to purify the land. No longer bored they sang and danced joyously in the red light of the flames."

But if, on the one hand, the force which took the American writer to Hollywood is a dark and inverted passion that makes him seek destruction in the arms of the blonde child whore, his corrupt and death-dealing sister, on the other hand, he is moved by a more beneficent love that takes him westward in search of an alien and unlikely father—more technician than artist, more businessman than creator—but a dreamer and peddler of dreams all the same, quite like himself. The relationship resembles that of Stephen Dedalus to Leopold Bloom in *Ulysses,* that blind man's word-bound book, which, after more than half a century, someone has been bold or foolish enough to try to make into a film; and as in Joyce's novel, so in our lives the mythical father of the artist in flight from tradition to Nightt wn is a Jew.

How oddly the love affair between the Gentile writer and the Jewish producer-director, the young philo-Semite and the aging Jew, emerges in our literature, which, as late as the twenties and on into the thirties, was continuing to portray chiefly anti-Semitic heroes and antipathetic Jewish foils, in the poetry of Pound and Eliot as well as in the prose of Dreiser and Sherwood Anderson and Hemingway and even Fitzgerald himself. But the latter—after the first rude shock of Hollywood, after the experience of confronting the Jews on their own home grounds, as it were, in a world where not they but the Gentile author seemed the intruder—learned to create an image of the Jew vastly different from the threatening bogeyman, Wolfsheim, who haunts the pages of *The Great Gatsby.* Monroe Stahr, the Jewish tragic hero of *The Last Tycoon,* the wary boy gang leader from the Bronx who has made himself top dog in Hollywood and is ready for destruction, represents for Fitzgerald not only a triumph of art but a victory over prejudice.

To *see* him, much less to love him was not easy for Fitzgerald, whose initial reaction, as recorded in "Crazy Sunday," was to find Hollywood's Jews funny, fit subjects only for burlesque. In that story he tells how his protagonist (himself, surely) begins at his first big movie party an intendedly hilarious takeoff "in the intonations of Mr. Silverstein": '—a story of divorce, the younger generators and the Foreign Legion. . . . But we got to build it up, see?. . . —then she says she feels this sex appil for him and he burns out and says, 'Oh, go on destroy yourself—' " But Fitzgerald's alter ego is greeted with boos and blank stares. "It was the resentment," the author explains, "of the community toward the stranger, the thumbs-down of the clan." And all, of course, played out in the house of that most eminent of doomed Jews, the figure which was to become eventually Monroe Stahr.

The word "Jew" is not mentioned, to be sure, any more than it is in Nathanael West's brief retelling of what may have been the very same incident, or one very like it, introduced as background conversation during a minor episode in *The Day of the Locust;* but this time we hear it in the voice of the "clan." " 'That's right,' said another man. 'Guys like that come out here, make a lot of money, grouse all the time about the place, flop on their assignments, then. . . tell dialect stories about producers they've never met.' " But when Fitzgerald attempts a full scale treatment of Stahr and his wife—the redemptive father-husband, and the dangerous actress-wife who were in real life Irving Thalberg and Norma Shearer—when he turns to them again in his unfinished novel, he is on top of his own Jewish problem, to the extent at least of being able to name names; registering what may have been his own first impressions in a detached and objective way, through the consciousness of a certain Prince Agge, who sitting at lunch with the executives of a great studio, notes: "They were the money men—they were the rulers. . . . Eight out of ten were Jews—. . . . As a turbulent man, serving his time in the Foreign Legion, he thought that Jews were too fond of their own skins. But he was willing to concede that they might be different in America under different circumstances, and certainly he found Stahr was much of a man in every way. . . ."

With Agge's final opinion the two spokesmen characters into whom Fitzgerald has split himself agree, Cecilia Brady, female and Irish and a worshipper of the great, loving Stahr unabashedly for his alien masculinity; and Wylie White, WASP presumably and tyro writer, admiring him for his control of the new narrative skills which make words seem obsolete. But *The Last Tycoon* remained unfinished and Stahr exits—or better, fades away—in a confusion of other loves: one of which Fitzgerald had borrowed for him out of his own life, exploiting his then current affair with Sheila Graham, who was herself, though not until years later, to exploit both his exploitation and the affair itself (not without the help of a ghost writer, of course) in a popular book, which, becoming a movie, brought Fitzgerald (not without the help of an actor, of course) back in triumph to the world of Hollywood from which he had died in despair. "There are no second acts in American lives," he had written in the notes to himself appended to the manuscript of *The Last Tycoon,* and "not one survived the castration." But he had forgotten about what was then still called "the silver screen."

No matter—for better or worse what exists of *The Last Tycoon* had fixed forever (or perhaps merely caught once and for all) a pattern which has been repeated over and over again in books as vastly different from each other as Christopher Isherwood's *Prater Violet,* Norman Mailer's *The Deer Park,* and Robert Penn Warren's *Flood.* Expatriate Englishman, wandering Jew, and transplanted Southern Agrarian, they portray each in his own way the romance of Celt or WASP writer and Jewish moviemaker, a sentimental allegory signifying the capitulation of High Art to Pop Art, not in terror, however, but in pity and affection. Isherwood, perhaps because he is confessedly a homosexual, is able to reveal the meaning of the encounter and the surrender with an uncustomary candor (though he, for reasons of his own, eschews the word "Jew"), permitting the one of his ill-matched pair who bears his own name to comment just before the novel's close: "Mother's Boy, the comic Foreigner with the funny accent. Well, that didn't matter. . . . For, beneath our disguises . . . we knew. Beneath outer consciousness, two other beings. . . had met and recognized each other, and had clasped hands. He was my father. I was his son. And I loved him very much."

But, of course, Isherwood's Herr Bergman, the director in flight from the Nazis and toward Hollywood, *is* a Jew—just as is Mailer's Charles Francis Eitel, in flight from Congressional Investigating Committees toward death, and even Robert Penn Warren's Yasha Jones, camouflaged behind an assumed last name and oddly at loose ends in the American Deep South. Yet each of these authors plays games with the deepest mythological identity of the adopted father, who represents to each the real maker of the movies for which they aspire to be given screen credits at least. Mailer is less coy and cagey about Eitel's origins in the dramatic version of *The Deer Park* than he was in the earlier novel; but even in the later work, Eitel when challenged admits only to being "half Jewish—on both sides" and in a context which makes it clear that he habitually lies about such matters. And though Brad Tolliver, the WASP-writer of

Warren's *Flood* would clearly love his director to be a Jew, the author will not grant him this mythological satisfaction—insisting that Yasha Jones is a "déraciné Georgian—. . . Georgia in Russia"; and when Brad says wistfully, "I thought you were a Jew," his longed-for foreign father answers oddly, "I sometimes think I am. . . . But we Georgians have a noble history, too."

Perhaps the problem arises in large part simply because, in the years since *The Last Tycoon,* the typical American novelist has ceased to be a provincial Gentile and has become himself an urban Jew; while the refugees to Hollywood (Daniel Fuchs, for instance and West himself) were already often Jewish even in Fitzgerald's own time—so that the contract of pre-Gutenberg Gentile and post-Gutenberg Jew was ceasing to be viable at the moment it was being first imagined. Yet how hard that mythological vision is to surrender even for Jews themselves, who, like Mailer, project *goyish* alter egos to represent their own entry into Hollywood; or, like Peter Viertel, invert the legendary romance—pitting a Jewish obsolescent writer against an Old Hollywood Pro turned super-Goy, or more precisely, maybe, super-Hemingway. Hemingway's name is, at any rate, often on the lips of Viertel's John Wilson, who views himself as having followed in the steps of the Master, only to go beyond by rendering the simplicity and silence which Hemingway pursued, in unspeaking images more appropriate than words. But maybe *all* Hollywood Pros tend to think of themselves as Hemingways, even the Jews, in a penultimate irony which demands that the gravediggers of books find a metaphor for their own lives in the career of a writer of books—who himself, in a more ultimate irony, defined his life style in imitation of that movie cowboy, Gary Cooper. Fitzgerald, certainly, whose own attitudes toward Hemingway were more complex than this, thought it all a sad joke, jotting down among his notes for the background of *The Last Tycoon:* "Tragedy of these men was that nothing in their lives had really bitten deep at all. Bald Hemingway characters."

Viertel's Hemingway-character is quite another matter, however, more like the author's flattering image of himself than Fitzgerald's wry vision of his bald imitators, a true communicant in the Church of Raw Experience and Mortal Danger, appropriately portrayed at play in the jungles of Africa. But he is no anti-Semite like the first Hemingway, this second one turned moviemaker; and he is shown choosing to insult the latterday Lady Brett of *White Hunter, Black Heart* rather than join her in vilification of the updated Robert Cohn, who is his companion and surrogate for the book's author. ". . . and suddenly the lady next to me," Wilson tells his own anti-Semitic lady-interlocutor, as his put-down begins, "and she was a beautiful lady, said that the one thing she didn't mind about Hitler was what he'd done to the Jews. Well, dear, I turned to her, and everyone was silent, and I said, 'Madam, I have dined with some ugly, goddamn bitches in my time. I've dined with some of the goddamnedest, ugliest bitches in the world, but you, dear, are the ugliest bitch of them all.' "

This is not just a pious political stand, a final development of Popular Front politics before it fades into general American liberalism, required of all men of good will after Hitler—though it is this in large part. It is also a declaration of allegiance to the movies themselves and the force that made them; since the movies *are* Jewish, after all: a creation of Jewish ingenuity and surplus Jewish capital, a by-product of the Jewish Garment Industry, which began by blurring away class distinctions in dress and ended by blotting out class distinctions in dreams. But the movies are, alas, ceasing to be Jewish, which is to say, they are dying—dying into something else.

These days there is scarcely a film produced which is not in fact an embryo T.V. program; its brief appearance in the neighborhood theater as clearly an intermediate step on the way to a lifelong run on the Late, Late Show—as the appearance in hard covers of a new book by, say, James Michener, has been for a long time an intermediate step to a film at that neighborhood theater. And (peace to Lenny Bruce, who first revealed to me the scope and depth of this distinction) as surely as chocolate is Jewish and fudge *goyish,* so are the movies Jewish and T.V. *goyish.* What the implications of this are beyond the fact that new mythologies of Pop Culture will have to be invented to suit new needs, and that the figure of the Jew is almost sure to be absent from them—I, the spiritual child of those Jewish Sages, Marx and Freud, leave to those sitting even now at the feet of *goyish* Gurus like Marshall McLuhan and Norman O. Brown.

Buffalo, N.Y.
—1967

A Night with Mr. Teas

THE IMMORAL MR. TEAS was approaching the end of a nine-month run at the little movie house in Seattle where I first saw it. Paired with it was *The Mouse that Roared,* a film I had accidentally seen twice before and one for which I have small affection. I am dismayed at its sentimental-liberal clichés espousing Love and deploring the Bomb. Naturally, I arrived too early and had to endure once more the final cuteness of "The Mouse," its technicolor reassurance that our world would survive—and that its survival would be an unmitigated Happy Ending. It was technicolor I really hated, I told myself; nothing could be true or good or beautiful in those never quite convincing tones, just as nothing could be high, wide, or handsome on the nonscale of the wide screen. "Justify God's ways to man—in color and VistaVision," I imagined the modern muse telling some new Milton; and foresaw the miserable event: four stars in the *Daily News,* ennui for any sensitive beholder.

Mr. Teas, however, turned out to be in technicolor, too—its opening all the vulgar tints of urban Southern California: a sun-dazzled city bus stop and our hero, briefcase in hand, beside a street-corner bench endorsed with an ad for a Jewish funeral home. Los Angeles and the undertakers again. Another cliché, I found myself thinking, the by-now-not-quite-fresh-or-moving metaphor for Hell in Our Time. And I was not reassured by the Monsieur Hulot-type music of the score—tinkle-jangle-tinkle, the submelody of city life, as Mr. Teas switched from bus to bike, changed from mufti to a pair of cerise-terra cotta overalls, and began to pedal along his insipid round of work: delivering false teeth to dentists' offices.

This at least was an apt metaphor, I argued with the self that wanted to get the hell out—a quite unhackneyed figure for a setting and routine as glistening and meaningless as death: the detached smile fixed in a polished vise. But one part of me still kept asking what I was doing there anyhow.

The last erotic picture I had been to see—also after a nine-month run—had been "Ecstasy"; but that had been some twenty-five or thirty years before, in another world. How different a world became clear quite soon, as I found myself laughing at a spectacle so antiromantic that it verged, for me, at least, on the anaphrodisiac. In *Mr. Teas* there was not only no passion, but no contact, no flesh touching flesh, no consummation shown or suggested. I remembered from the earlier film the pearls slipping from Hedy Lamarr's throat, her face blurred in the ecstasy advertised by the title. For pornography the woman's angle of vision is necessary, but here were no women outside of Bill Teas's head; and Bill Teas was nobody's dreamed lover, only a dreamer, with his half-modest, half-comical beard, his sagging pectoral muscles, his little lump of a belly creased by baggy shorts or hidden by overalls.

And Mr. Teas could touch no one—not in lust or love or in the press of movement along a street. Once in the film he lays his hand on flesh, the shoulder of an eight-year-old girl working out with a hula hoop, and she beans him with a rock. Any really nubile, desirable female is doomed to disappear into the ladies' room or the arms of some lover whose face we never see—as unreal, finally, as the girl he embraces. Mr. Teas conducts his odd business and carries his frustrated dreams through a world of noncontact and noncommunication.

In his wanderings from office to office, from home to lunchroom, the violently overalled Mr. Teas finds occasional refreshment in staring down the more than half-revealed bosoms of receptionists, waitresses, and cashiers. In his otherwise quite arid world, all females are singularly and lushly *décolleté,* as if they existed chiefly to titillate his impotent desire, and as the plot unfolds with all the step-by-step deliberateness of a strip tease, Mr. Teas is shown developing a talent for imaginarily stripping ever closer to the buff the girls who torment him on his rounds. An injection in a dentist's chair from an assistant, whose breasts become in fantasy the headrest which supports him, helps Mr. Teas create the first of his visions; but awake and undrugged, he continues to fabricate them, finally comes to regard them as a disease from which he asks a psychiatrist to deliver him.

The visions of Mr. Teas are, however, strange in a way which at first we do not notice, because their strangeness is an accepted part of a world in which we all live. That is to say, the nudity he creates is never *complete* nudity. Sitting, for instance, in a café, gnawing on an obscenely large slab of watermelon, Mr. Teas finds that the waitress who serves him has become quite naked, except for the merest doily of an apron covering the meeting place of thighs and belly. Admiring the nonchalance of Mr. Teas as he gnaws his cool fruit and pretends to ignore the feast beside him, we realize that the joke has adapted to the conditions which make the showing of the film possible: there must be an apron; he must not touch her.

It is not finally just a matter of observing certain rules of the censors, but of making those very rules the subject of the picture, the butt of its jokes. For what we are shown when the rules are observed is not female flesh, but pin-up pictures—moving pictures of moving pin-up pictures, life twice removed; and this is why *Mr. Teas,* funny as it is (and it *is* funny—chiefly because of the discretion of its cameraman, Russ Meyers, and the skill with which Bill Teas projects the impassive, dogged, low-keyed lust of its *schlemiel*-hero), is also a quite serious film. It is not merely like the strip tease, the candy-box cover, the girlie calendar, and the fold-out magazine nude; it is about them.

In one sequence, during which he presumably searches for escape at the beach, Mr. Teas stumbles on a professional photographer who is running through her paces a model or hopeful starlet, first in an ultimate bikini, then stripped of her bra and finally clothed only in the surf. How icily the girl simulates the poses of lewd appeal, wild abandon, and sexual allure, though for the camera only and on cue as the camera clicks. Meanwhile, Mr. Teas, too, has a camera, a miniature Brownie that cannot compete with the equipment of the professional any more than the meager personal dreams of Mr. Teas can compete with those professionally produced. He inhabits a world of prefabricated fantasies, stumbling into one situation after another in which those fantasies are being manufactured for men powerless to evoke for themselves even the intangible shadow of sex.

We are, therefore, constantly being reminded of how we, too, live in a world where, whatever the natural bent of our desires, we are forced by billboards, night clubs, stage entertainments, cartoons, and photographs, by the very ads which assail us for brassieres and Kleenex and Pepsi-Cola, into playing the Peeping Tom; and of how we, too, are not only teased by the ten thousand commercially produced provocations, but become finally our own teasers—stripping but not possessing (not even in the deepest imagination), as we have been taught. There is one unforgettable scene, in which, as Mr. Teas aimlessly walks down a street, a window shade springs up and, plastered almost against the pane, a female body is revealed from just below the shoulders to just above the waist—a noseless face in which the nipples make wide eyes above the pursed, tiny mouth of the navel; a face which seems to stare back at the starer, as if all flesh (not only male flesh, as our convention demands) had become eyes and the only communication in either direction were peeping.

As the picture draws to a close, we follow Mr. Teas on a day's outing to a lake, where he is after the same game as always, though by now he has become terrified by his talent, thinks he flees what he seeks; and he finds it. This time there is not just a single girl, but four at once, who, quite naked, rock themselves on hammocks, dip and splash in the shallow water or swim where it is deeper, row boats, and toss a ball, while Mr. Teas ogles and spies, smiling his half-beatific, half-idiotic smile, and separated from them still, as if by the invisible glass pane of the TV toothpaste commercial.

So stylized, so indistinguishable from mass-produced fantasies in every premeditated, robotic gesture are the girls he watches that it is difficult to tell whether the whole episode is intended to be taken for an actual event or merely the most extended of Mr. Teas's dreams. Certainly what of the audience remained to the end the night I first saw the movie (several more clean-cut pairs of college sweethearts had walked out early in the game) argued about it vehemently from either side. But the point, I suppose, lies really in this ambiguity, this irreality. And just as the girls were, in their gestures, more the fabrications of mass culture than of nature, so they were also in their dimensions and their textures. It is impossible to remember, two days after leaving the theater, what color their hair was.

These girls do not quite seem to be women, adapted as they are to the mythical dimensions of pin-ups and to a more than mythical smoothness of texture. Nowhere is there pimple or blemish or sagging skin or untoward wrinkle or mottled flesh. The loving, patient camera (not really a moviemaker's camera at all, but that of the still photographer) that follows the play of light and shade on haunch and hollow finds no human imperfection, not even goose flesh or beads of sweat. Such girls seem more like fruit than flesh— hothouse fruit, serenely perfect and savorless, not to be touched or eaten. Only looked at. Unreal. Unreal. Unreal. This is the sadness of *Mr. Teas.*

As old restrictions crumble in our society, the naked flesh assumes its proper place among the possible subjects for movies, the place it has always held in the other, less public arts; but meanwhile, in the United States, we have been long corrupted by the pseudo-arts of tease and titillation, conditioned to a version of the flesh more appropriate for peeking than love or lust or admiration or even real disgust. In European films like *Room at the Top* or *Hiroshima, Mon Amour,* we have been offered newer versions of nudity appropriate to serious art, versions of a nudity not so much seen as felt, responded to in tenderness and desire. Whether equivalent versions will prove possible in American films seems to me doubtful; perhaps our way will have to be comic rather than passionate or even sentimental. If this is so, *Mr. Teas,* for all its lapses into the obvious, may someday seem a pioneering effort. Its makers have not attempted to surmount the difficulties which confront the American moviemaker who desires to make nakedness his theme; but they have, with absolute good humor, managed at once to bypass and to illuminate those difficulties. The end result is a kind of imperturbable comedy, with overtones of real pathos.

How especially stupid in light of all this are the cuts demanded by the censors of New York, who, in deleting some twenty minutes, have eliminated not only the nipples and buttocks they were obviously after but also the wit and pathos and point of *Mr. Teas.* To

New York moviegoers I am moved to say: Stay away from what will be called *The Immoral Mr. Teas* in your theaters. It will be a tease in the worst sense of the word, the merest leering hint, the dullest remnant of a once witty film—a joke of its own kind on public standards of decency. Decency! How hard it is to believe that the names of those involved in the production are not anticipatory jokes which this final one fulfills. But DeCenzie is apparently the actual name of the producer of the film, Bill Teas that of the chief actor, and Cantlay the real name of a real California street. It pays to be lucky!

I do not know whether the makers of *Mr. Teas* were merely lucky or really aware of the implications of the movie they were making; and New York viewers will have no way of deciding for themselves without a trip to Atlantic City, where an uncut version is being shown. Perhaps DeCenzie and Russ Meyers, the cameraman, are themselves only two more victims of the process which reduces sex in America to sex in the eye, and are critics of the process only inadvertently. I have been reading press releases about how Russ Meyers, who shot *Mr. Teas* in four days at the cost of only twenty-four thousand dollars and dreams of earning a million on it, has produced another film, another bareback quickie, called *Eve and the Handyman*. Maybe from the start he has just been cashing in on the new freedom which provides new ways of exploiting the mindless audience. I would like to believe that this is not so, that he knew all along not merely how funny but how sad *Mr. Teas* really was. In the end, it doesn't matter. The artist is entitled to whatever can be found in his work. I hope he makes the million.

—1959

FIVE

The Death of *Avant-Garde* Literature

THAT WE HAVE been living through the death of *avant-garde* literature over the past couple of decades most of us now know. What we are still trying to find out is how to come to terms with that fact, beyond deploring or applauding it, or, in stoical despair, simply refusing to do either. We would scarcely feel at such a loss if we confronted merely the rejection by certain leading authors of advanced or experimental art, for this has been customary in America. Certainly our greatest writers of the 1920's began their careers precisely by turning their backs on the extremes of modernism to woo the mass audience through the mass magazines. Scott Fitzgerald, we remember, was at home in the *Saturday Evening Post* from the start, and that same magazine opened its arms to Faulkner at the very moment he was contemplating *Absalom, Absalom!;* while Hemingway, after a brief flirtation with the little magazines and a vicious parody of their modes in *Torrents of Spring,* headed via *Esquire* toward the maximum audience provided by *Life.* Fair enough. Such adjustments are in the American grain; even Henry Miller has become at last a garrulous, platitudinous old man, and a tourist attraction to boot.

But our major novelists have customarily placed themselves *against* an *avant-garde* tradition which flourishes elsewhere, in Europe or in certain peripheral writers of our own—Djuna Barnes, for example, or Gertrude Stein. They have consciously chosen another direction. Now, alas, there is no choice. The European gravediggers of the *avant-garde,* whether talented survivors of the times of *tran-*

sition, like Samuel Beckett, or slick young counterfeiters of the experimental, like Robbe-Grillet, do not constitute a counterforce sufficient to make newer ambitious middlebrows like, say, Harvey Swados or John Cheever seem either desperately inept or rewardingly reactionary.

But neither does membership in the academy contrived of yesterday's *avant-gardism,* the nostalgic imitation of techniques revolutionary and exciting in the heyday of James Joyce, produce a literature advanced for us. The very youngest among us may think so briefly, of course, since they are disposed to regard kindly the pioneers of modernism without really knowing them; and it is to such readers that academically "advanced" journals like the *Evergreen Review* are likely to seem less intolerably dull than they in fact are. Such readers, too (and they can be of all ages), have helped, surely, in giving to the warmed-over Proustianism of Durrell's Alexandrian books the cachet of *avant-garde.* What is fashionable, however, cannot properly claim the rewards appropriate to the antifashionable; no writer can have the rewards of book-club adoption and of alienation at the same time.

With the aid of the mass media, antifashion becomes fashion among us at a rate that bewilders critics and writers alike; and nobody will find so many staunch friends and supporters as the man who labels himself an outcast or an enemy of society. A pair of public figures like Arthur Miller and Tennessee Williams illustrate the situation with all the grossness that pertains to the commercial theater; but their tragicomedy of accepted alienation is played out monthly, with a little more verve and grace, in the pages of ladies' magazines, like *Vogue* and *Harper's Bazaar,* or in the sophisticated slicks, like *Esquire.*

No techniques can be devised these days, at any rate, for which the literature major (trained in some Ivy League haven by a highbrow, defeated or biding his time) is not appallingly well prepared; or toward which his wife (who, with the years, does more and more of his reading for him) is not dishearteningly well-disposed. But the literature major and his wife, along with the second-generation literature majors who are their children, constitute the new middlebrow audience, whose appearance testifies to the technical exhaustion of the *avant-garde.* Certainly the devices which once characterized such art (the fractured narrative line, stream-of-consciousness, insistent symbolism, ironic allusion) seem today more banal than the well made plot, the set description, the heavy-handed morality that they were invented to displace. The whole meaning of advanced art was never contained, however, in mere technique, which was only one of the many modes of offending the philistine reader.

It is, after all, *offense* on many fronts which distinguishes *avant-garde* from other kinds of writing. Lowbrow or frankly unadventurous art asks of its readers *identification,* trying to persuade them that it speaks their language, the language of all but a handful of snobs, and embodies their values, the values of all but a handful of nuts. Middlebrow or pretentiously vacuous art offers as its hallmark *protest,* trying to persuade its readers that they are joined with the author and an enlightened not-too-few in a gallant struggle against some quite unambiguous evil, sponsored only by members of the Other Side: slavery, McCarthyism, anti-Semitism, cruelty to dogs or children, The Bomb. Its techniques, therefore, are intended to create neither a private language nor a public one, but only the jargon of a party, in power and defending itself, or out and trying to get in.

Highbrow or truly experimental art aims at *insult;* and the intent of its typical language is therefore exclusion. It recruits neither defenders of virtue nor opponents of sin; only shouts in the face of the world the simple slogan, *épater le bourgeois,* or "mock the middle classes," which is to say, mock most, if not quite all, of its readers. Once the highbrow could offend such readers simply by sporting a contempt for syntax and capital letters, like e. e. cummings, or merely by displaying too much anxiety over the intricacies of writing well, like Henry James. But such easy strategies are no longer available to us, in a time when even journalists have learned to sham a concern with style, and even college rhetorics teach toleration of deviant mechanics and grammar.

No, if offense is still to be given, the good burghers still to be bugged, it must be done by ideas and not by techniques, a program of action rather than an aesthetic code. But what ideas remain offensive in a time in which not merely grammars and dictionaries, but guide books for raising children and for living the good life insist that everything is relative and to know all is to forgive all? Once the advocacy of alcohol and sex, drunkenness and adultery was enough to enrage the respectable; but the long fight to drink and make love as one pleases, memorialized in hundreds of books since the first lost generation announced its lostness in *The Sun Also Rises,* has passed by way of the cocktail party and the fifty-minute hour with the psychiatrist into polite society. *The Sun Also Rises* has ceased being a dangerous book to become a required one, a bore assigned in class; and the mass arts complete the degradation mass education begins, making it next an O.K., which is to say, very bad, movie.

With what a sense of daring, however, the hitherto dirty word "impotent" was first spoken aloud in that film. Yet how quickly we have come to accept since more and more formerly forbidden words: "whore" and God knows what, allowing them first, of course, in foreign films, then in ill-lighted, low-budget domestic ones, i.e., art films (needing some guaranty that old taboos are being broken in the name of something higher than mere entertainment), then, at last, in commercial films themselves. Who a couple of decades ago would have thought the brutal sexual humor of Billy Wilder possible in neighborhood theaters, or the horror-pornography of Tennessee Williams?

It is not that we Americans have given up our hatred and fear of sex, on which indeed our very sense of our selves and our ties with the past depend; it is only that we now expect, even demand, that our traditional distaste be spoken aloud in four-letter words rather than whispered in genteel polysyllables. Think of the success of J. D. Salinger, in whom sex is consistently presented as a temptation or threat to his teen-age saints—of Holden Caulfield fleeing seduction in classrooms and elevators and hotel rooms, and of Franny crying out in effect, "I'd rather have a nervous breakdown than sleep with you, dear!" In any event, we listen these days to both sides, as they say, even on the level of the popular arts; and both sides speak the same language—a language against which only a diminishing minority of ever more comical bigots cries out in protest.

And what, then, is the serious writer to do in his search for occasions for offense now that the rank and file have overrun his old positions? How can he shock those who, when they do not agree with him, tolerate him? He can, of course, raise the ante higher and higher, *i.e.,* advocate more and more sex, polygamy compounded to hypergamy; or strip it of sentimentality, making the orgasm itself rather than anything called love the goal; or describe more and more closely, with attention to more and more senses, and in language less and less clinical or idyllic, the act itself. He can become, that is to say, Norman Mailer or Jack Kerouac, but he cannot keep the new middlebrows from loving him.

Still he pleases rather than offends, sells well rather than being ignored, returns home to find not the cops waiting for him, but the photographers from *Life,* and a delegation of students inviting him to lecture to their class at City College. Mailer produces what has been described as the conscience literature of the present $30,000-a-year ex-radicals; and Kerouac provides fantasies for the future $40,000-a-year ex-Beatniks. Only in night clubs can the grossest language or the sternest contempt for banal morality stir up the police (so that if giving offense be the hallmark of the *avant-garde,* Lenny Bruce is the last *avant-garde* artist in America); between the covers of books, hard or soft, anything goes—at least with that growing public that ransacks the past for banned novels and stops in the supermarket between groceries and cigarettes to pick up *Fanny Hill* or D. H. Lawrence or the *Kama Sutra.* Already the time is in sight when the only forbidden book will be *Little Women.*

Does anything at all then shock the enlightened middlebrow as he stands, Martini in hand, Freud on shelf, and the slogans of yesterday's *avant-garde* turned to platitudes in his mouth? For a little while at least, it seemed as if homosexuality and drug-taking provided for him the *frisson* proper to *avant-garde* art. Did not even the most emancipated of his own teachers shudder when confronted for the first time by a generation of students crying out, "Freud is a fink!"—meaning that they preferred not to make *ego* of *id,* rationality of impulse, but to extend the range of waking consciousness with the aid of the hallucinogens: peyote or marijuana or LSD? Did not his own even more emancipated wife tremble hearing for the first time the sons of her fellow members in the League of Women Voters insist that they wanted not more and freer sex with more and freer girls, but each other?

Certainly, in response to these new possibilities of offense, a new literature arose, best exemplified, perhaps, by the novels of William Burroughs, *Naked Lunch* and *The Soft Machine,* and the poetry of Allen Ginsberg, particularly *Howl;* though a figure of greater mythical potency than either, perhaps, is Jean Genet—"St. Genet," who has been lucky enough to have Jean-Paul Sartre as his St. Paul. These laureates of homosexual love and drug-taking have set themselves the task not merely of offending the most tolerant, but of redeeming for them some sense of the real horror of a world they so peacefully and self-righteously contemplate, programs of reform in hand. The nightmare reality created by Genet and Burroughs out of their own fantasies and obsessions, their flirtation with madness and contempt for the rational, defies tolerance and reform alike. It is tempting to dismiss their work as mere scare literature, play-terror; but they evoke a vision of the end of man as we have conceived him from the time of the Greeks to the age of Freud—surely terror genuine enough for anyone.

But how quickly their breakthrough to new frontiers of offense has been followed up by imitators and vulgarizers. In our time of rapid communication, the first discoverers have scarcely staked out a territory before the tourists have come, then the carpetbaggers, and at last the middlebrow suburbanites—eager to set up housekeeping on prime sites overlooking the first landing places. So Burroughs' lonely island has turned into a suburb—complete with writer's clubs and home courses in creative writing; so his kind of *avant-garde* has become *Kitsch.* In how few years we have lived to see a popular subliterature made on the model of his *Naked Lunch* and Genet's *Our Lady of the Flowers,* the creation of a new genre recounting the adventures of the homosexual prostitute in nighttown, a kind of *Adventures of Freddie Hill*—since it is really Fanny's brother rather than Fanny herself who interests us.

Her trials and triumphs have begun to seem, indeed, a little dull, too normal to titillate or appall any but the dullest middlebrows passing an idle hour in bus stations or airports. Perhaps John Rechy's recent *City of Night* (described on the jacket as "dealing with the little-known world of hidden sex") represents as well as anything the subsidence of a newer sort of pornography into a newer sort of *Kitsch,* the latest rapid transformation of *avant-garde* art to everybody's entertainment. We can interpret, surely, the end to which his hero comes as symbolic for us all, since he returns from "the clandestine world of furtive love" to childhood and mother and Texas, where the weary clichés of magazine fiction for ladies rise up in his mind; and he leaves us (as if it were *Woman's Day* we had been reading) with the plaint of a small boy for his dog: "And the fierce wind is an echo of angry childhood and of a very scared boy looking out the window—remembering my dead dog outside by the wounded house and thinking: It isn't fair! *Why can't dogs go to Heaven?"* But when will the moving picture version be made?

—1964

Cross the Border—Close the Gap

To DESCRIBE the situation of American letters at the end of the sixties is difficult indeed, almost impossible, since the language available to critics at this point is totally inappropriate to the best work of the artists who give the period its special flavor, its essential life. But precisely here is a clue, a way to begin: not with some presumed crisis of poetry or fiction, but with the unconfessed scandal of contemporary literary criticism, which for three or four decades now has vainly attempted to deal in terms invented to explain, defend, and evaluate one kind of book with *another* kind of book—so radically different that it calls the very assumptions underlying those terms into question. Established critics may think that they have been judging recent literature; but, in fact, recent literature has been judging them.

Almost all living readers and writers are aware of a fact which they have no adequate words to express, not in English certainly, nor even in American. We are living, have been living for two decades—and have become acutely conscious of the fact since 1955 —through the death throes of Modernism and the birth pangs of Post-Modernism. The kind of literature which had arrogated to itself the name Modern (with the presumption that it represented the ultimate advance in sensibility and form, that beyond it newness was not possible), and whose moment of triumph lasted from a point just before World War I until one just after World War II, is *dead,* i.e., belongs to history not actuality. In the field of the novel, this means that the age of Proust, Mann, and Joyce is over; just as in verse that of T. S. Eliot, Paul Valéry, Montale and Seferis is done with.

61

Obviously *this* fact has not remained secret: and some critics have, indeed, been attempting to deal with its implications. But they have been trying to do it in a language and with methods which are singularly inappropriate, since both method and language were invented by the defunct Modernists themselves to apologize for their own work and the work of their preferred literary ancestors (John Donne, for instance, or the *symbolistes),* and to educate an audience capable of responding to them. Naturally, this will not do at all; and so the second or third generation New Critics in America, like the spiritual descendants of F. R. Leavis in England (or the neo-neo-Hegelians in Germany, the belated Croceans in Italy), end by proving themselves imbeciles and naïfs when confronted by, say, a poem of Allen Ginsberg, a new novel by John Barth.

Why not, then, invent a New New Criticism, a Post-Modernist criticism appropriate to Post-Modernist fiction and verse? It sounds simple enough—quite as simple as imperative—but it is, in fact, much simpler to say than do; for the question which arises immediately is whether there can be *any* criticism adequate to Post-Modernism. The Age of T. S. Eliot, after all, was the age of a literature essentially self-aware, a literature dedicated, in avowed intent, to analysis, rationality, anti-Romantic dialectic—and consequently aimed at eventual respectability, gentility, even, at last, academicism. Criticism is natural, even essential to such an age; and to no one's surprise (though finally there were some voices crying out in dismay), the period of early twentieth-century Modernism became, as it was doomed to do, an Age of Criticism: an age in which criticism began by invading the novel, verse, drama, and ended by threatening to swallow up all other forms of literature. Certainly, it seems, looking back from this point, as if many of the best books of the period were critical books (by T. S. Eliot and Ezra Pound and I. A. Richards, by John Crowe Ransom and Kenneth Burke and R. P. Blackmur, to mention only a few particularly eminent names); and its second-best, novels and poems eminently suited to critical analysis, particularly in schools and universities: the works of Proust-Mann-and-Joyce, for instance, to evoke a trilogy which seems at the moment more the name of a single college course than a list of three authors.

We have, however, entered quite another time, apocalyptic, antirational, blatantly romantic and sentimental; an age dedicated to joyous misology and prophetic irresponsibility; one, at any rate, distrustful of self-protective irony and too great self-awareness. If criticism is to survive at all, therefore, which is to say, if criticism is to remain or become useful, viable, relevant, it must be radically altered from the models provided by Croce or Leavis or Eliot or Erich Auerbach, or whoever; though not in the direction indicated by Marxist critics, however subtle and refined. The Marxists are last-ditch defenders of rationality and the primacy of political fact, intrinsically hostile to an age of myth and passion, sentimentality and fantasy.

On the other hand, a renewed criticism certainly will no longer be formalist or intrinsic; it will be contextual rather than textual, not primarily concerned with structure or diction or syntax, all of which assume that the work of art "really" exists on the page rather than in a reader's passionate apprehension and response. Not words-on-the-page but words-in-the-world or rather words-in-the-head, which is to say, at the private juncture of a thousand contexts, social, psychological, historical, biographical, geographical, in the consciousness of the lonely reader (delivered for an instant, but an instant only, from all of those contexts by the *ekstasis* of reading): this will be the proper concern of the critics to come. Certain older critics have already begun to provide examples of this sort of criticism by turning their backs on their teachers and even their own earlier practices. Norman O. Brown, for instance, who began with scholarly, somewhat Marxian studies of Classic Literature has moved on to metapsychology in *Life Against Death* and *Love's Body*; while Marshall McLuhan, who made his debut with formalist examinations of texts by Joyce and Gerard Manley Hopkins, has shifted to metasociological analyses of the mass media in *Understanding Media,* and finally to a kind of pictographic shorthand, half put-on and half serious emulation of advertising style in *The Medium is the Message.*

The voice as well as the approach is important in each case, since neither in Brown nor McLuhan does one hear the cadence and tone proper to "scientific" criticism of culture, normative psychology or sociology attached to literary texts. No, the pitch, the rhythms, the dynamics of both are mantic, magical, more than a little *mad* (it is a word, a concept that one desiring to deal with contemporary literature must learn to regard as more honorific than

pejorative). In McLuhan and Brown—as in D. H. Lawrence earlier, Charles Olson when he first wrote on Melville—a not so secret
fact recently hushed up in an age of science and positivism is can-
didly confessed once more: criticism is literature or it is nothing.
Not amateur philosophy or objective analysis, it differs from other
forms of literary art in that it starts not with the world in general
but the world of art itself, in short, that it uses one work of art as
an occasion to make another.

There have been, of course, many such meditating works of art
in the past, both fairly recent (Nietzsche's *Birth of Tragedy)* and
quite remote (Longinus *On The Sublime),* which make it clear that
the authority of the critic is based not on his skills in research or his
collection of texts but on his ability to find words and rhythms and
images appropriate to his ecstatic vision of, say, the plays of Euripides or the opening verses of *Genesis.* To evoke Longinus or even
Nietzsche, however, is in a sense misleading, suggesting models too
grandiose and solemn. To be sure, the newest criticism must be aesthetic, poetic in form as well as substance; but it must also be, in
light of where we are, comical, irreverent, vulgar. Models have appeared everywhere in recent years but tentatively, inadvertently as
it were—as in the case of Angus Wilson, who began a review of
City of Night some years ago (in the pages of an ephemeral little
magazine), by writing quite matter-of-factly, "Everyone knows
John Rechy is a little shit." And all at once we are out of the
Eliotic church, whose dogmas, delivered *ex cathedra,* two generations of students were expected to learn by heart: "Honest criticism
and sensitive appreciation are directed not upon the poet but upon
the poetry. . . . The mind of the mature poet differs from that of
the immature one not precisely on any valuation of personality, not
by being necessarily more interesting, or having 'more to say,' but
rather by being a more finely perfected medium in which etc., etc."

Unless criticism refuses to take itself quite so seriously or at
least to permit its readers not to, it will inevitably continue to reflect
the finicky canons of the genteel tradition and the depressing pieties
of the Culture Religion of Modernism, from which Eliot thought
he had escaped—but which in fact he only succeeded in giving a
High Anglican tone: "It is our business as readers of literature, to
know what we like. It is our business, as Christians, *as well as* read-

ers of literature, to know what we ought to like." But not to know that such stuff is funny is to be imprisoned in Church, cut off from the liberating privilege of comic sacrilege. It is high time, however, for such sacrilege rather than such piety; as some poets have known really ever since Dada, without knowing how to keep their sacrilege from becoming itself sacred; as the dearest obscenities of Dada were sanctified into the social "art" of Surrealism under the fell influence of Freud and Marx.

The kind of criticism which the age demands is, then, Death-of-Art Criticism, which is most naturally practiced by those who have come of age since the death of the "New Poetry" and the "New Criticism." But it ought to be possible under certain conditions to some of us oldsters as well, even those of us whose own youth was coincident with the freezing of all the madness of *symbolisme*-Dada-*surréalisme* into the rigidities of academic *avant-garde*. In this sense, the problem of the aging contemporary critic is quite like that of the no-longer-young contemporary novelist, which one necessarily begins to define even as he defines the dilemma of the critic.

In any case, it seems evident that writers not blessed enough to be under thirty (or thirty-five, or whatever the critical age is these days) must be reborn in order to seem relevant to the moment, and those who inhabit it most comfortably, i.e., the young. But no one has even the hope of being reborn unless he knows first that he is dead—dead, to be sure, for someone else; but the writer exists as a writer precisely for someone else. More specifically, no novelist can be reborn until he knows that insofar as he remains a novelist in the traditional sense, he is dead; since the traditional novel is dead—not dying, but dead. What was up to only a few years ago a diagnosis, a predication (made, to be sure, almost from the moment of the invention of the novel: first form of pop literature, and therefore conscious that as compared to classic forms like epic or tragedy its life span was necessarily short) is now a fact. As certainly as God, i.e., the Old God, is dead, so the Novel, i.e., the Old Novel, is dead. To be sure, certain writers, still alive and productive (Saul Bellow, for instance, or John Updike, Mary McCarthy or James Baldwin), continue to write Old Novels, and certain readers, often with a sense of being quite up-to-date, continue to read them. But so do preachers continue to preach in the Old Churches, and congregations gather to hear them.

It is *not* a matter of assuming, like Marshall McLuhan, that the printed book is about to disappear, taking with it the novel—first form invented for print; only of realizing that in all of its forms—and most notably, perhaps, the novel—the printed book is being radically, functionally altered. No medium of communication ever disappears merely because a new and more efficient one is invented. One thinks, for instance of the lecture, presumably superannuated by the invention of moveable type, yet flourishing still after more than five centuries of obsolescence. What is demanded by functional obsolescence is learning to be less serious, more frivolous, a form of *entertainment*. Indeed, it could be argued that a medium begins to be felt as entertainment only at the point where it ceases to be a necessary or primary means of communication, as recent developments in radio (the total disappearance, for instance, of all high-minded commentators and pretentious playwrights) sufficiently indicates. Students at any rate are well aware of this truth in regard to the university lecture, and woe to the lecturer (of whom, alas, there are many) who does not know it!

In any event, even as the "serious" lecture was doomed by the technology of the fifteenth century, and the "serious" church service by the philology of the eighteenth and nineteenth—so is the "serious" novel, and "serious" criticism as well, by the technology and philology of the twentieth. Like the lecture and Christian church services, its self-awareness must now include the perception of its own absurdity, even impossibility. Since, however, the serious novel of our time is the Art Novel as practiced by Proust, Mann, and Joyce and imitated by their epigones, it is that odd blend of poetry, psychology, and documentation, whose real though not always avowed end was to make itself canonical, that we must disavow. Matthew Arnold may have been quite correct in foreseeing the emergence of literature as scripture in a world which was forsaking the Old Time Religion: but the life of the New Scriptures and the New Time Religion was briefer than he could have guessed.

Before the Bible of the Christians and Jews ceased to be central to the concerns of men in Western society, it had become merely a "book" among others; and this, indeed, may have misled the Arnoldians, who could not believe that a time might come when not merely *the* Book ceased to move men, but even books in general. Such, however, is the case—certainly as far as all books which consider themselves "art," i.e., scripture once removed, are concerned; and for this reason the reborn novel, the truly new New Novel must be anti-art as well as antiserious. But this means, after all, that it must become more like what it was in the beginning, more what it seemed when Samuel Richardson could not be taken *quite* seriously, and what it remained in England (as opposed to France, for instance) until Henry James had justified himself as an artist against such self-declared "entertainers" as Charles Dickens and Robert Louis Stevenson: popular, not quite reputable, a little dangerous—the one his loved and rejected cultural father, the other his sibling rival in art. The critical interchange on the nature of the novel to which James contributed "The Art of Fiction" and Stevenson "A Humble Remonstrance" memorializes their debate —which in the thirties most readers believed had been won hands down by James's defense of the novel as art; but which in the dawning seventies we are not sure about at all—having reached a time when *Treasure Island* seems somehow more to the point and the heart's delight than, say, *The Princess Casamassima.*

This popular tradition the French may have understood once (in the days when Diderot praised Richardson extravagantly, and the Marquis de Sade emulated him in a dirtier book than the Englishman dared) but they long ago lost sight of it. And certainly the so-called *"nouveau roman"* is in its deadly earnest almost the opposite of anything truly new, which is to say, anti-art. Robbe-Grillet, for example, is still the prisoner of dying notions of the *avantgarde;* and though he is aware of half of what the new novelist must do (destroy the Old, destroy Marcel Proust), he is unaware of what he must create in its place. His kind of antinovel is finally too arty and serious: a kind of neo-neo-classicism, as if to illustrate once more that in the end this is all the French can invent no matter how hard they try. Re-imagined on film by Alain Resnais, *Last Year at Marienbad* speaks to the young; but in print it remains merely *chic,* which is to say, a fashionable and temporary error of taste. Better by far, and by the same token infinitely more pertinent is Samuel Beckett, who having been born Irish rather than French, finds it hard to escape being (what some of his readers choose to ignore) compulsively and hilariously funny.

Best of all, however, and therefore totally isolated on the recent French scene (except for the perceptive comments of that equally ambiguous figure, Raymond Queneau) is Boris Vian, especially in his most successful work of fiction, *L'écume des jours,* recently translated into English as *Mood Indigo.* Indeed, Boris Vian is in many ways a prototype of the New Novelist, though he has been dead for a decade or so and his most characteristic work belongs to the years just after World War II. He was, first of all, an Imaginary American (as even writers born in the United States must be these days), who found himself in total opposition to the politics of America at the very moment he was most completely immersed in its popular culture—actually writing a detective novel called *I Will Spit On Your Grave* under the pen name of Vernon Sullivan, but pretending that he was only its translator into French. In fact, by virtue of this peculiar brand of mythological Americanism he managed to straddle the border, if not quite close the gap between high culture and low, belles-lettres and pop art. On the one hand, he was the writer of pop songs and a jazz trumpeter much influenced by New Orleans style; and on the other, the author of novels in which the thinly disguised figures of such standard French intellectuals as Jean Paul Sartre and Simone de Beauvoir are satirized. But even in his fiction, which seems at first glance quite traditional or, at any rate, conventionally *avant-garde,* the characters move toward their fates through an imaginary city whose main thoroughfare is called Boulevard Louis Armstrong.

Only now, however, has Vian won the audience he all along deserved, finding it first among the young of Paris, who know like their American counterparts that such a closing of the gap between elite and mass culture is precisely the function of the Novel Now— not merely optional as in Vian's day, but necessary. And though most of the younger American authors who follow a similar course follow it without ever having known him, by a shared concern rather than direct emulation, he seems more like them than such eminent American forerunners of theirs as Faulkner or Hemingway (except perhaps in Hemingway's neglected early burlesque, *Torrents of Spring,* and Faulkner's self-styled "pot-boiler," *Sanctuary.)*

Vian, unfortunately, turned to the form of the Pop Novel only for the work of his left hand, to which he was not willing even to sign his own name, writing in *L'écume des jours* what seems superficially a traditional enough love story to disarm the conventional critics; though it is finally undercut by a sentimentality which redeems its irony, and reflects a mythology too Pop and American for neo-neo-Classicists to bear.

The young Americans who have succeeded Vian, on the other hand, have abandoned all concealment, and when they are most themselves, nearest to their central concerns, turn frankly to Pop forms—though not, to be sure, the detective story which has by our time become hopelessly compromised by middlebrow condescension: an affectation of college professors and presidents. The forms of the novel which they prefer are those which seem now what the hard-boiled detective story once seemed to Vian: at the furthest possible remove from art and *avant-garde,* the greatest distance from inwardness, analysis, and pretension; and, therefore, immune to lyricism, on the one hand, or righteous social commentary, on the other. It is not compromise by the market place they fear; on the contrary, they choose the genre most associated with exploitation by the mass media: notably, the Western, Science Fiction, and Pornography.

Most congenial of all is the Western, precisely because it has for many decades now seemed to belong exclusively to pulp magazines, run-of-the mill T.V. series and Class B movies, which is to say, has been experienced almost purely as myth and entertainment rather than as "literature" at all—and its sentimentality has, therefore, come to possess our minds so completely that it can now be mitigated without essential loss by parody, irony—and even critical analysis. In a sense, our mythological innocence has been preserved in the Western, awaiting the day when, no longer believing ourselves innocent in fact, we could decently return to claim it in fantasy. But such a return to the Western represents, of course, a rejection of laureates of the loss of innocence like Henry James and Hawthorne: those particular favorites of the forties, who despite their real virtues turn out to have been too committed to the notion of European high art to survive as major influences in an age of Pop. And it implies as well momentarily turning aside from our beloved Herman Melville (compromised by his New Critical admirers and the countless Ph.D. dissertations they prompted), and even from Mark Twain. To Hemingway, Twain could still seem central to a living tradition, the Father of us all, but being Folk rather than Pop in essence, he has become ever more remote from an urban, industrialized world, for which any evocation of pre-Civil War, rural America seems a kind of pastoralism which complements rather than challenges the Art Religion. Folk Art knows and accepts its place in a class-structured world which Pop blows up, whatever its avowed intentions. What remains are only the possibilities of something closer to travesty than emulation—such a grotesque neo-Huck, for instance, as the foulmouthed D. J. in Norman Mailer's *Why Are We in Vietnam,* who, it is wickedly suggested, may *really* be a Black joker in Harlem pretending to be the White refugee from respectability. And, quite recently, Twain's book itself has been rewritten to please and mock its exegetes in John Seelye's *Huck Finn for The Critics,* which lops off the whole silly-happy ending, the deliverance of Nigger Jim (in which Hemingway, for instance, never believed) and puts back into the tale the cussing and sex presumably excised by the least authentic part of Samuel Clemens' mind—as well as the revelation at long last, that what Huck and Jim were smoking on the raft was not tobacco but "hemp," which is to say, marijuana. Despite all, however, Huck seems for the moment to belong not to the childhood we all continue to live, but to the one we have left behind.

Natty Bumppo, on the other hand, dreamed originally in the suburbs of New York City and in Paris, oddly survives along with his author. Contrary to what we had long believed, it is James Fenimore Cooper who now remains alive, or rather who has been reborn, perhaps not so much as he saw himself as in the form D. H. Lawrence re-imagined him en route to America; for Cooper understood that the dream which does not fade with the building of cities, but assumes in their concrete and steel environment the compelling vividness of a waking hallucination, is the encounter of Old World men and New in the wilderness, the meeting of the transplanted European and the Red Indian. No wonder Lawrence spoke of himself as "Kindled by Fenimore Cooper."

The Return of the Redskin to the center of our art and our deep imagination, as we all of us have retraced Lawrence's trip to the mythical America, is based not merely on the revival of the oldest and most authentic of American Pop forms, but also projects certain meanings of our lives in terms more metapolitical than political, which is to say, meanings valid as myth is valid rather than as history. Writers of Westerns have traditionally taken sides for or against the Indians; and unlike the authors of the movies which set the kids to cheering at the Saturday matinees of the twenties and thirties, the new novelists have taken a clear stand with the Red Man. In this act of mythological renegacy they have not only implicitly declared themselves enemies of the Christian Humanism, but they have also rejected the act of genocide with which our nation began—and whose last reflection, perhaps, is to be found in the War in Vietnam.

It is impossible to write any Western which does not in some sense glorify violence; but the violence celebrated in the anti-White Western is guerrilla violence: the sneak attack on "civilization" as practiced first by Geronimo and Cochise and other Indian warrior chiefs, and more latterly apologized for by Ché Guevara or the spokesman for North Vietnam. Warfare, however, is not the final vision implict in the New Western, which is motivated on a deeper level by a nostalgia for the Tribe: a form of social organization thought of as preferable both to the tight two-generation bourgeois family, from which its authors come, and the soulless out-of-human-scale bureaucratic state, into which they are initiated via schools and universities. In the end, of course, both the dream of violence in the woods and the vision of tribal life, rendered in terms of a genre that has long been the preferred reading of boys, seems juvenile, even infantile. But this is precisely the point; for what recommends the Western to the New Novelist is pre-eminently its association with children and the kind of books superciliously identified with their limited and special needs.

For the German, brought up on Karl May, the situation is quite similar to that in which the American, who grew up with Cooper or his native imitators, finds himself. What has Old Shatterhand to do with Art, asks the one, even as the other asks the same of Chingachgook. And the answer is *nothing*. The legendary Indians have nothing to do with Art in the traditional sense, everything to do with joining boy to man, childhood to adulthood, immaturity to maturity. They preside over the closing of the Gap which aristocratic conceptions of art have opened between what fulfills us at eight or ten or twelve and what satisfies us at forty or fifty or sixty.

In light of all this, it is perhaps time to look again at the much-discussed "immaturity" of American literature, the notorious fact that our classic books are boy's books—our greatest novels at home in the Children's Section of libraries; in short, that they are all in some sense "Westerns": accounts of an idyllic encounter between White man and Non-White in one or another variety of wilderness setting. But suddenly this fact—once read as a "flaw" or "failure" or "lack" (it implies, after all, the absence in our books of heterosexual love and of the elaborate analysis of social relations central to the Continental novel)—seems evidence of a real advantage, a clue to why the Gap we now want to close opened so late and so unconvincingly, as it were, in American letters. Before Henry James, none of our novelists felt himself cut off from the world of magic and wonder; he had only to go to sea or, especially, to cross our own particular Border, the Frontier, to inhabit a region where adults and children, educated and uneducated, shared a common enchantment.

How different the plight of mid-nineteenth-century English writers, like Lewis Carroll or Edward Lear or George Macdonald, who had to pretend that they were writing exclusively for the nursery in order to enter the deep wonderland of their own imaginations. Even in our own time, a writer like J. R. R. Tolkien found it necessary to invent the Hobbits in a book specifically aimed at children, before he could release the fearful scholarship (another device foreign to American mythologies) and presumably adult magic of the Rings Trilogy. It makes a difference, after all, whether one thinks of the World Across The Border as Faerie or Frontier, fantasy or history. It has been so long since Europeans lived their deepest dreams—but only yesterday for us. And this is why even now, when we are at last sundered from those dreams, we can turn rotten-ripe without loss of essential innocence, be (what has become a model for the young of all the world, as Godard's *Weekend* testifies) decadent children playing Indians; which is to say, imaginary Americans, all of us, whether native to this land or not. But to be an American (unlike being English or French or whatever) is precisely to *imagine* a destiny rather than to inherit one; since we have always been, insofar as we are Americans at all, inhabitants of myth rather than history—and have now come to know it.

In any case, our best writers have been able to take up the Western again—playfully and seriously at once, quite like their ancestors who began the Revolution which made us a country by playing Indians in deadly earnest and dumping all that English Tea into the salt sea that sundered them from their King. There are many writers still under forty, among them the most distinguished of their generation, who have written New Westerns which have found the hearts of the young, particularly in paperback form; since to these young readers, for reasons psychological as well as economic, the hardcover book with its aspiration to immortality in libraries begins to look obsolete. John Barth's *The Sotweed Factor* represents the beginning of the wave that has been cresting ever since 1960 and that has carried with it not only Barth's near contemporaries like Thomas Berger (in *Little Big Man),* Ken Kesey (in both *One Flew Over the Cuckoo's Nest* and *Sometimes a Great Notion),* and most recently Leonard Cohen (in his extraordinarily gross and elegant *Beautiful Losers)*—but has won over older and more established writers like Norman Mailer whose newest novel, *Why Are We in Vietnam?,* is not as its title seems to promise a book about a War in the East as much as a book about the idea of the West. Even William Burroughs, expert in drug fantasies and homosexual paranoia, keeps promising to turn to the genre, though so far he has contented himself with another popular form, another way of escaping from personal to public or popular myth, of using dreams to close rather than open a gap: Science Fiction.

Science Fiction does not seem at first glance to have as wide and universal appeal as the Western, in book form at least, though perhaps it is too soon to judge, for it is a very young genre, indeed, having found itself (after tentative beginnings in Jules Verne, H. G. Wells etc.), its real meaning and scope, only after World War II. At that point, two things become clear: first, that the Future was upon us, that the pace of technological advance had become so swift that a distinction between Present and Future would get harder and harder to maintain; and second, that the End of Man, by annihilation or mutation, was a real, even an immediate possibility. But these are the two proper subjects of Science Fiction: the Present Future and the End of Man—not time travel or the penetration of outer space, except as the latter somehow symbolize the former.

Perhaps only in quite advanced technologies which also have a tradition of self-examination and analysis, bred by Puritanism or Marxism or whatever, can Science Fiction at its most explicit, which is to say, expressed in words on the page, really flourish. In any case, only in America, England, and the Soviet Union does the Science Fiction Novel or Post-Novel seem to thrive, though Science Fiction cartoon strips and comic books, as well as Science Fiction T.V. programs and especially films (where the basic imagery is blissfully wed to electronic music, and words are kept to a minimum) penetrate everywhere. In England and America, at any rate, the prestige and influence of the genre are sufficient not only to allure Burroughs (in *Nova Express*), but also to provide a model for William Golding (in *Lord of the Flies*), Anthony Burgess (in *The Clockwork Orange*), and John Barth (whose second major book, *Giles Goatboy*, abandoned the Indian in favor of the Future).

Quite unlike the Western, which asserts the difference between England and America, Science Fiction reflects what still makes the two mutually distrustful communities one; as, for instance, a joint effort (an English author, an American director) like the movie *2001: A Space Odyssey* testifies. If there is still a common "Anglo-Saxon" form, it is Science Fiction. Yet even here, the American case is a little different from the English; for only in the United States is there a writer of first rank whose preferred mode has been from the first Science Fiction in its unmitigated Pop form. Kurt Vonnegut, Jr., did not begin by making some sort of traditional bid for literary fame and then shift to Science Fiction, but was so closely identified with that popular, not-quite-respectable form from the first, that the established critics were still ignoring him completely at a time when younger readers, attuned to the new rhythm of events by Marshall McLuhan or Buckminster Fuller, had already made underground favorites of his *The Sirens of Titan* and *Cat's Cradle*. That Vonnegut now, after years of neglect, teaches writing in a famous American university and is hailed in lead reviews in the popular press is a tribute not to the critics' acuity but to the persuasive powers of the young.

The revival of pornography in recent days, its moving from the periphery to the center of the literary scene, is best understood in this context, too; for it, like the Western and Science Fiction, is a form of Pop Art—ever since Victorian times, indeed, the *essential* form of Pop Art, which is to say, the most unredeemable of all kinds of subliterature, understood as a sort of entertainment closer to the pole of Vice than that of Art. Many of the more notable recent works of the genre have tended to conceal this fact, often because the authors themselves did not understand what they were after, and have tried to disguise their work as earnest morality (Herbert Selby's *Last Exit to Brooklyn,* for instance) or parody (Terry Southern's *Candy).* But whatever the author's conscious intent, all those writers who have helped move Porn from the underground to the foreground have in fact been working toward the liquidation of the very conception of pornography; since the end of Art on one side means the end of Porn on the other. And that end is now in sight, in the area of films and Pop songs and poetry, but especially in that of the novel which seemed, initially at least, more congenial than other later Pop Art forms to the sort of private masturbatory reverie which is essential to pornography.

It is instructive in this regard to reflect on the careers of two publishers who have flourished extraordinarily because somehow they sensed early on that a mass society can no longer endure the distinction between low literature and a high, especially in the area of sex; and that the line drawn early in the century between serious, "artistic" exploitation of pornography (e.g., *Lady Chatterley's Lover),* and so-called "hard-core" pornography was bound to be blurred away. Even the classics of the genre straddle the line: *Fanny Hill,* for example, and de Sade's *Justine,* as do more recent works like John Rechy's *City of Night* or Stephen Schneck's *The Night Clerk,* whose sheer dirtiness may be adulterated by sentiment or irony but remains a chief appeal. This, at any rate, Maurice Girodias and Barney Rosset appear to have sensed; and from both sides of the Atlantic they have, through the Olympia Press and Grove Press, supplied the American reading public, chiefly but not exclusively the young, with books (including, let it be noted, Nabokov's *Lolita,* the sole work in which the pursuit of Porn enabled that emigré writer to escape the limitations of early twentieth-century *avant-garde)* exploiting, often in contempt of art and seriousness, not just Good Clean Sex, but sadism, masochism, homosexuality, coprophilia, necrophilia etc. etc.

The standard forms of heterosexual copulation, standardly or "poetically" recorded, seem oddly old-fashioned, even a little ridiculous; it is *fellatio,* buggery, flagellation that we demand in order to be sure that we are not reading Love Stories but Pornography. A special beneficiary of this trend has been Norman Mailer, whose first novel, *The Naked and the Dead,* emulated the dying tradition of the anti-war art novel, with occasional obscenities thrown in, presumably in the interest of verisimilitude. But more and more, Mailer has come to move the obscenity to the center, the social commentary to the periphery, ending in *Why Are We in Vietnam?* with an insistence on foul language and an obsession with scatology which are obviously ends in themselves, too unremitting to be felt as merely an assault on old-fashioned sensibility and taste. And even in his earlier Pop Novel, *An American Dream,* which marked his emergence from ten years in which he produced no major fiction, he had committed himself to Porn as a way into the region to which his title alludes: the place where in darkness and filth all men are alike—the Harvard graduate and the reader of the *Daily News,* joined in fantasies of murdering their wives and buggering their maids. To talk of such books in terms of Dostoevski, as certain baffled critics have felt obliged to do, is absurd; James Bond is more to the point. But to confess this would be to confess that the old distinctions are no longer valid, and that critics will have to find another claim to authority more appropriate to our times than the outmoded ability to discriminate between High and Low.

Even more disconcertingly than Mailer, Philip Roth has with *Portnoy's Complaint* raised the question of whether "pornography," even what was called until only yesterday "hard-core pornography" any longer exists. Explicit, vulgar, joyous, gross and pathetic all at once, Roth has established himself not only as the laureate of masturbation and oral-genital lovemaking but also as a master of the "thin" novel, the novel with minimum inwardness—ironically presented as a confession to a psychiatrist. Without its sexual interest, therefore, the continual balancing off of titillation and burlesque— his book has no meaning at all, no more than any other dirty joke, to which genre it quite clearly belongs. There is pathos, even terror in great plenty, to be sure, but it is everywhere dependent on, subservient to the dirty jokes about mothers, Jews, shrinks, potency, impotency; and Roth is, consequently, quite correct when he asserts that he is less like such more solemn and pious Jewish-American writers as Saul Bellow and Bernard Malamud, than he is like the half-mad pop singer Tiny Tim (himself actually half-Arab and half-Jew).

"I am a Jew Freak," Roth has insisted, "not a Jewish Sage"— and one is reminded of Lennie Bruce, who was there first, occupying the dangerous DMZ between the world of the stand-up comedian and that of the proper maker of fictions. But Bruce made no claim to being a novelist and therefore neither disturbed the critics nor opened up new possibilities for prose narrative. Indeed, before *Portnoy's Complaint,* the Jewish-American novel had come to seem an especially egregious example of the death of belles-lettres, having become smug, established, repetitive and sterile. But *Portnoy* marks the passage of that genre into the new world of Porn and Pop, as Roth's booming sales (even in hardcover!) perhaps sufficiently attest.

It is, of course, the middle-aged and well-heeled who buy the hardcover editions of the book; yet their children apparently are picking it up, too, for once not even waiting for the paperback edition. They know it is a subversive book, as their parents do not (convinced that a boy who loves his mother can't be all bad), and as Roth himself perhaps was not at first quite aware either. Before its publication, he had been at least equivocal on the subject of frankly disruptive literature; full of distrust, for instance, for Norman Mailer—and appears therefore to have became a Pop rebel despite himself, driven less by principle than by a saving hunger for the great audience, quite like that which moved John Updike recently out of his elitist exile toward best-sellerdom and relevance in *Couples.*

There is, however, no doubt in the minds of most other writers whom the young especially prize at the moment that their essential task is to destroy once and for all—by parody or exaggeration or grotesque emulation of the classic past, as well as by the adaptation and "camping" of Pop forms just such distinctions and discriminations. But to turn High Art into vaudeville and burlesque at the same moment that Mass Art is being irreverently introduced into museums and libraries is to perform an act which has political as well as aesthetic implications: an act which closes a class, as well as a generation gap. The notion of one art for the "cultured," i.e., the favored few in any given society—in our own chiefly the university educated—and another subart for the "uncultured," i.e., an excluded majority as deficient in Gutenberg skills as they are untutored in "taste," in fact represents the last survival in mass industrial societies (capitalist, socialist, communist—it makes no difference in this regard) of an invidious distinction proper only to a class-structured community. Precisely because it carries on, as it has carried on ever since the middle of the eighteenth century, a war against that anachronistic survival, Pop Art is, whatever its overt politics, *subversive:* a threat to all hierarchies insofar as it is hostile to order and ordering in its own realm. What the final intrusion of Pop into the citadels of High Art provides, therefore, for the critic is the exhilarating new possibility of making judgments about the "goodness" and "badness" of art quite separated from distinctions between "high" and "low" with their concealed class bias.

But the new audience has not waited for new critics to guide them in this direction. Reversing the process typical of Modernism —under whose aegis an unwilling, aging elite audience was bullied and cajoled slowly, slowly, into accepting the most vital art of its time—Post-Modernism provides an example of a young, mass audience urging certain aging, reluctant critics onward toward the abandonment of their former elite status in return for a freedom the prospect of which more terrifies than elates them. In fact, Post-Modernism implies the closing of the gap between critic and audience, too, if by critic one understands "leader of taste" and by audience "follower." But most importantly of all, it implies the closing of the gap between artist and audience, or at any rate, between professional and amateur in the realm of art.

The jack of all arts is master of none—professional in none, and therefore no better than any man jack among the rest of us, formerly safely penned off from the practitioners we most admire by our status as "audience." It all follows logically enough. On the one hand, a poet like Ed Sanders, or a novelist like Leonard Cohen grows weary of his confinement in the realm of traditional high art; and the former organizes a musical Pop Group called the Fugs, while the latter makes recordings of his own Pop songs to his own guitar accompaniment. There are precedents for this, after all, not only as in the case of Boris Vian, which we have already noticed, but closer to home: in the career, for instance, of Richard Farina, who died very young, but not before he had written that imperfect, deeply moving novel, *Been Down So Long It Looks Like Up to Me,* and had recorded a song or two for the popular audience.

Meanwhile, even more surprisingly some who had begun, or whom we had begun to think of, as mere "entertainers," Pop performers without loftier pretensions, were crossing the line from their direction. Frank Zappa, for example, has in interviews and in a forthcoming book insisted on being taken seriously as poet and satirist, suggesting that the music of his own group, The Mothers of Invention, has been all along more a deliberate parody of Pop than an extension of it in psychedelic directions; while Bob Dylan, who began by abandoning Folk Music with left-wing protest overtones in favor of electronic Rock and Roll, finally succeeded in creating inside that form a kind of Pop surrealist poetry, passionate, mysterious, and quite complex; complex enough, in fact, to prompt a score of scholarly articles on his "art." Most recently, however, he has returned to "acoustic" instruments and to the most naïve traditions of country music—apparently out of a sense that he had grown too "arty," and had once more to close the gap by backtracking across the border he had earlier lost his first audience by crossing. It is a spectacular case of the new artist as Double Agent.

Even more spectacular, however, is that of John Lennon, who coming into view first as merely one of the Beatles, then still just another rock group from Liverpool, has revealed himself stage by stage as novelist, playwright, movie maker, guru, sculptor, etc., etc. There is a special pathos in his example since, though initially inspired by American models, he has tried to work out his essentially American strategies in English idioms and in growing isolation on the generally dismal English scene. He has refused to become the prisoner of his special talent as a musician, venturing into other realms where he has, initially at least, as little authority as anyone else; and thus provides one more model for the young who, without any special gift or calling, in the name of mere possibility insist on making all up and down America, and, more tentatively perhaps, everywhere else in the world, tens of thousands of records, movies, collections of verse, paintings, junk sculptures, even novels, in complete contempt of professional "standards." Perhaps, though, the novel is the most unpromising form for an amateur age (it is easier to learn the guitar or make a two-minute eight-millimeter film), and it may be doomed to become less and less important, less and less central, no matter how it is altered. But for the moment at least, on the border between the world of Art and that of non-Art, it flourishes with especial vigor in proportion as it realizes its transitional status, and is willing to surrender the kind of "realism" and analysis it once thought its special province in quest of the marvelous and magical it began by disavowing.

Samuel Richardson may have believed that when he wrote *Pamela* and *Clarissa* he was delivering prose fiction from that bondage to the *merveilleux* which characterized the old Romances; but it is clear now that he was merely translating the Marvelous into new terms, specifically, into bourgeois English. It is time, at any rate, to be through with pretenses; for to Close the Gap means also to Cross the Border between the Marvelous and the Probable, the Real and the Mythical, the world of the boudoir and the counting house and the realm of what used to be called Faerie, but has for so long been designated mere madness. Certainly the basic images of Pop forms like the Western, Science Fiction and Pornography suggest mythological as well as political or metapolitical meanings. The passage into Indian Territory, the flight into Outer Space, the ecstatic release into the fantasy world of the orgy: all these are analogues for what has traditionally been described as a Journey or Pilgrimage (recently we have been more likely to say "Trip" without altering the significance) toward a transcendent goal, a moment of Vision.

But the mythologies of Voyage and Vision which the late Middle Ages and the Renaissance inherited from the Classical World and the Judaeo-Christian tradition, and which froze into pedanticism and academicism in the eighteenth and nineteenth century, have not survived their last ironical uses in the earlier part of the twentieth: those burlesque-pathetic evocations in Joyce's *Ulysses,* Eliot's *The Waste Land,* Mann's *Joseph and His Brothers* or the *Cantos* of Ezra Pound. If they are not quite dead, they should be, *need* be for the health of post-Art—as, indeed, Walt Whitman foresaw, anticipating the twenty-first century from the vantage point of his peculiar vision more than a hundred years ago.

> Come Muse migrate from Greece and Ionia,
> Cross out please those immensely overpaid accounts,
> That matter of Troy and Achilles' Wrath, and Aeneas'
>   Odysseus' wanderings,
> Place "Removed" and "To Let" on the rocks of your
>   snowy Parnassus,
> Repeat at Jerusalem . . .

Pop Art, however, can no more abide a mythological vacuum than can High Art: and into the space left vacant by the disappearance of the Matter of Troy and the myths of the ancient Middle East has rushed, first of all, the Matter of Childhood: the stuff of traditional fairy tales out of the Black Forest, which seems to the present generation especially attractive, perhaps, because their "progressive" parents tended to distrust it. But something much more radically new has appeared as well: the Matter of Metropolis and the myths of the Present Future, in which the nonhuman world about us, hostile or benign, is rendered not in the guise of elves or dwarfs or witches or even Gods, but of Machines quite as uncanny as any Elemental or Olympian—and apparently as immortal. Machines and the mythological figures appropriate to the media massproduced and mass-distributed by machines: the newsboy who, saying SHAZAM in an abandoned subway tunnel, becomes Captain Marvel; the reporter (with glasses), who shucking his civilian garb in a telephone booth is revealed as Superman, immune to all but Kryptonite—these are the appropriate images of power and grace for an urban, industrial world busy manufacturing the Future.

But the Comic Book heroes do not stand alone. Out of the world of Jazz and Rock, of newspaper headlines and political cartoons, of old movies immortalized on T.V. and idiot talk shows carried on car radios, new anti-Gods and anti-Heroes arrive, endless wave after wave of them: "Bluff'd not a bit by drainpipe, gasometer, artificial fertilizers," (the appropriate commentary is Whitman's), "smiling and pleas'd with palpable intent to stay"—in our Imaginary America, of course. In the heads of our new writers, they live a secondary life, begin to realize their immortality: not only Jean Harlow and Marilyn Monroe and Humphrey Bogart, Charlie Parker and Louis Armstrong and Lennie Bruce, Geronimo and Billy the Kid, the Lone Ranger and Fu Manchu and the Bride of Frankenstein, but Hitler and Stalin, John F. Kennedy and Lee Oswald and Jack Ruby as well; for the press mythologizes certain public figures, the actors of Pop History, even before they are dead —making a doomed President one with Superman in the Supermarket of Pop Culture, as Norman Mailer perceived so accurately and reported so movingly in an essay on John F. Kennedy.

But the secret he told was already known to scores of younger writers at least, and recorded in the text and texture of their work. In the deep memory of Leonard Cohen writing *Beautiful Losers,* or Richard Farina composing *Been Down So Long It Looks Like Up to Me,* or Ken Kesey making *Sometimes a Great Notion,* there stir to life not archetypal images out of books read in school or at the urging of parents; but those out of comic books forbidden in schools, or radio and T.V. programs banned or condescendingly endured by parents. From the taboo underground culture of the kids of just after World War II comes the essential mythology which informs the literature of right now. As early as T. S. Eliot, to be sure, jazz rhythms had been evoked, as in "O O O O that Shakesperherian Rag—It's so elegant, So intelligent . . .," but Eliot is mocking a world he resents; and even in Brecht's *Three Penny Opera,* the emulation of Pop music seems still largely "slumming." In the newest writers, however, mockery and condescension alike are absent, since they are not slumming; they are living in the only world in which they feel at home. They are able, therefore, to recapture a certain rude magic in its authentic context, by seizing on myths not as stored in encyclopedias or preserved in certain beloved ancient works—but as apprehended at their moment of making, which is to say, at a moment when they are not yet labeled "myths."

In some ways the present movement not only in its quest for myths, but also in its preference for sentimentality over irony, and especially in its dedication to the Primitive, resembles the beginnings of Romanticism, with its yearning for the Naïve, and its attempt to find authentic sources for poetry in folk forms like the *Märchen* or the ballads. But the Romantics returned exclusively toward the Past in the hope of renewal—to a dream of the Past, which they knew they could only write, not actually live. And, indeed, there persists in the post-Modernists some of that old nostalgia for folk ways and folk-rhythms, curiously tempered by the realization that the "folk songs" of an electronic age are made not in rural loneliness or in sylvan retreats, but in superstudios by boys singing into the sensitive ear of machines—or even by those machines themselves editing, blending, making out of imperfect scraps of human song an artifice of simplicity only possible on tape. What recent writers have learned, and are true enough children of the Present Future to find exhilarating, is not only that the *Naïve* can be machine produced, but that dreams themselves can be manufactured, projected on T.V. or Laser beams with all the vividness of the visions of Saints. In the first wave of Romanticism, pre-electronic Romanticism, it took an act of faith on the part of Novalis to be able to say, "Life is not a dream, but it can be and probably should be made one." And echoing his German producer, in the pages of both *Lilith* and *Phantastes,* George Macdonald, maddest of the Victorian mad visionaries, echoes the tone of desperate hope. But to the young in America, who have learned to read Macdonald once more, along with his English successors, Charles Williams and C. S. Lewis and Tolkien, the declaration of faith has become a matter of fact.

The Dream, the Vision, *ekstasis:* these have again become the avowed goals of literature; for our latest poets realize in this time of Endings, what their remotest ancestors knew in the era of Beginnings, that merely "to instruct and delight" is not enough. Like Longinus, the new novelists and critics believe that great art releases and liberates as well; but unlike him, they are convinced that wonder and fantasy, which deliver the mind from the body, the body from the mind, must be naturalized to a world of machines— subverted perhaps or even transformed, but certainly not destroyed or denied. The ending of Ken Kesey's *One Flew Over the Cuckoo's*

Nest expresses fictionally, metaphorically, that conviction, when the Indian who is his second hero breaks out of the Insane Asylum in which "The System" has kept him impotent and trapped—and flees to join his fellows who are building a fishing weir on a giant hydro-electric power dam. The Dam and Weir both are essential to post-electronic Romanticism, which knows that the point is no longer to pursue some uncorrupted West over the next horizon, since there is no incorruption and all our horizons have been reached. It is rather to make a thousand little Wests in the interstices of a machine civilization, and, as it were, on its steel and concrete back; to live the tribal life among and with the support of machines; to shelter new communes under domes constructed according to the technology of Buckminster Fuller; and warm the nakedness of New Primitives with advanced techniques of solar heating.

All this is less a matter of choice than of necessity because, it has turned out, machine civilization tends inevitably to synthesize the primitive, and *ekstasis* is the unforeseen end of advanced technology, mysticism the by-product—no more nor no less accidental in penicillin—of scientific research. In the antiseptic laboratories of Switzerland, the psychedelic drug LSD was first developed, first tried by two white-coated experimenters; and even now Dow Chemical which manufactures napalm also produces the even more powerful psychedelic agent STP. It is, in large part, thanks to machines—the supermachines which, unlike their simpler proto-types, insist on tending us rather than demanding we tend them— that we live in the midst of a great religious revival, scarcely noticed by the official spokesmen of established Christian churches since it speaks quite another language. Yet many among us feel that they are able to live honestly only by what machines cannot do better than they—which is why certain poets and novelists, as well as pop singers and pornographic playwrights, are suggesting in print, on the air, everywhere, that not Work but Vision is the proper activity of men, and that, therefore, the contemplative life may, after all, be preferable to the active one. In such an age, *our* age, it is not surprising that the books which most move the young are essentially religious books, as, indeed, pop art is always religious.

In the immediate past, however, when an absolute distinction was made between High Art and Pop, works of the latter category tended to be the secret scriptures of a kind of shabby, store-front church—a religion as exclusive in its attempt to remain the humble possession of the unambitious and unlettered, as the canonical works of High Art in their claim to be an esoteric Gospel of art itself, available only to a cultivated elite. But in a time of Closing the Gap, literature becomes again prophetic and universal—a continuing revelation appropriate to a permanent religious revolution, whose function is precisely to transform the secular crowd into a sacred community: one with each other, and equally at home in the world of technology and the realm of wonder. Pledged like Isaiah to speaking the language of everyone, the prophets of the new dispensation can afford to be neither finicky nor genteel; and they echo, therefore, the desperate cry of the Hebrew prototype: "I am a man of unclean lips in the midst of a people of unclean lips."

Let those to whom religion means security beware, for it is no New Established Church that is in the process of being founded; and its communicants are, therefore, less like the pillars of the Lutheran Church or Anglican gentlemen than they are like ranters, enthusiasts, Dionysiacs, Anabaptists: holy disturbers of the peace of the devout. Leonard Cohen, in a moment of vision which constitutes the climax of *Beautiful Losers,* aptly calls them "New Jews"; for he sees them as a saved remnant moving across deserts of boredom, out of that exile from our authentic selves which we all share, toward a salvation none of us can quite imagine. Such New Jews, Cohen (himself a Jew as well as a Canadian) adds, do not have to be Jewish but probably do have to be Americans—by which he must surely mean "Imaginary Americans," since, as we have been observing all along, there were never any other kind.

—1970

SEVEN

In Quest of George Lippard

GEORGE LIPPARD, the author of *The Quaker City,* or *The Monks of Monk Hall,* is a little-known figure in the history of American literature. For many years, as a matter of fact, his very existence was kept a secret in the official histories of the novel in the United States, as if he represented a shameful episode in a past we were all doing our best to forget. In recent years, however, scholarly candor has triumphed over patriotic shame; and beginning with Alexander Cowie in *The Rise of the American Novel* (1948), historians of our fiction have been making an effort to come to terms with Lippard and his "dirty" book.

It is, after all, impossible to ignore forever a writer who produced one of the all-time best-sellers, a book which he himself boasted "has been more attacked, and more read, than any work of American fiction ever published"; and which, in fact, sold 60,000 copies in 1844, the year of publication, and was still being bought at the rate of 30,000 a year in 1854, the year of Lippard's death. Not only in America, but in England and on the Continent, Lippard was read by those who pretended to be scandalized as well as by those who didn't even realize that they ought to be shocked. In Germany the "most immoral work of the age" seems to have been a special favorite; and, ironically, during the period when *The Quaker City* had disappeared from our own literary histories, it continued to be listed in German ones as the work of Friedrich Gerstäcker under the title *Die Quackerstadt und ihre Geheimnisse.*

Lippard is an immensely attractive figure, a revolutionary dandy who, in the short thirty-two years of his life, managed to

dazzle and provoke the Philadelphia society in which he moved, ro-
mantically wrapped in a Byronic cape and always armed against
paid assassins whom he imagined everywhere. Brought up to be a
minister, he found no church liberal enough to suit his beliefs, and
became a kind of lay apostle preaching the doctrine of socialism.
All forms and conventions of the community in which he lived
seemed to him intolerable; and he married his wife, for instance, by
the simple process of taking her hand as they stood together on a
high rock overlooking his native city.

He was not only an immensely prolific novelist, author of innu-
merable books, *The Legends of the American Revolution, Blanche
of Brandywine, The Mysteries of Florence, The Memoirs of a
Preacher, The Empire City, The Bank Director's Son, The En-
tranced, New York: Its Upper Ten,* etc.; he was a lecturer as well
and fancied himself a natural political leader. He founded, in fact, a
radical organization called The Brotherhood of Union (later
renamed The Brotherhood of America), of which he appointed himself the "Supreme Washington"; and he issued revolutionary mani-
festos insisting "When Labor has tried all other means in vain—
. . . then we advise Labor to go to War . . . War with the
Rifle, Sword and Knife!" Moreover, he considered his fiction another weapon to be used in the struggle. "LITERATURE merely considered as an ART is a despicable thing. . . . A literature which
does not work practically, for the advancement of social
reform . . . is just good for nothing at all." But this, surely, is one
clue to Lippard's long eclipse.

Had he been just a "dirty" writer, he might have survived
change of fashion and critical neglect, survived as an underground
classic; and had he been a properly pious socialist, his memory
might well have been preserved by Marxist critics in search of literary ancestors. To be a "dirty" socialist writer, however, is to lose
on all counts. Yet Lippard does not stand alone in his allegiance,
on the one hand, to sensation and smut, and, on the other, to social
reform. Indeed, to come to terms with him we must come to terms
with a whole school of fiction which the habit of contempt and the
limitations of our own hopelessly elitist views of art have made it
difficult for us to understand. Outside the context of that stream of
literature, Lippard can only seem an eccentric, a freak, rather than

one of the group of literary pioneers who first tried to create a true popular literature.

It is tempting to see Lippard in an American setting, which is to say, one too parochial really to explain him; and, as a matter of fact, he himself encourages us to do so. His most famous novel is dedicated to Charles Brockden Brown, to whom he also wrote a moving tribute in a contemporary magazine; and his name, otherwise excluded from respectable notice, was associated in literary history with Edgar Allen Poe, whom he befriended. What is easier, then, and superficially more satisfactory than to associate him with these two exponents of the American Gothic, both of whom had connections of one kind or another with Lippard's native Philadelphia.

Lippard is, however, very different indeed from either of his two fellow countrymen, not only in his resolve to address a mass audience rather than to woo an elite one, and in the slapdash style and open form he felt suitable for that end—but in theme and setting as well. It is the city which concerns him, the contemporary American city, New York and Philadelphia in particular; and he therefore rejects equally the brand of exoticism that moved Poe to set many of his dream-fugues against a half-imaginary European background, and that which impelled Brockden Brown (as well as Poe in his single novel) to evoke the shadowy terror of the American wilderness.

In order to find writers whom he really resembles, one has to look beyond rather than before him on the American scene—to Jack London, Theodore Dreiser, and Norman Mailer[1], for instance, who, like him, combine a taste for the sentimental and sensational with an ideological commitment to socialism. Dreiser, moreover, shares with him an appalled fascination with the city and its depraved masters, though he rather lacks what Lippard, London, and Mailer possess in an eminent degree—a kind of natural access to the erotic dreams and paranoid fantasies of the male members of the working class.

---

[1] Mailer's *An American Dream* seems, in fact, closer to what Lippard was doing in *The Quaker City* than anything written between, and this is, perhaps, because it was written serially and under pressure for a popular magazine. If only it had been illustrated as well!

Poe, on the other hand, touches the imagination of childhood, appealing to what remains most childlike in us and thus creating fantasies appropriate to the impotence of that state, as opposed to those arising out of the deprivations of the poor. It is perhaps because the child tends to dream of withdrawing from the world which excludes him, triumphing over it in proud loneliness, rather than of making it in that world like the workingman, that Poe—despite having helped invent so basic a pop form as the detective story —has become a founding father of *avant-garde* literature intended for an elite audience. The descendants of Poe are French dandies, not American radicals—Baudelaire and Mallarmé rather than London and Dreiser and Mailer.

It is finally, however, not even Lippard's American successors, much less his predecessors, who provide the essential clue to what he is after, but certain of his contemporaries in England and Europe: in particular, the popular German novelist Friedrich Gerstäcker (1816–1872), the English publisher, journalist, and writer of fiction G. W. M. Reynolds (1814–1879); and, especially, that super best-seller in a time of best-sellers, the French novelist Eugène Sue (1804–1857). All three of these novelists, along with Lippard himself, were responding to the special challenges of their period, as were, in their own way, their more respectable contemporaries like Dickens and Balzac; and like the latter they aimed at commercial success before critical acclaim.

In the case of Gerstäcker, Reynolds, Sue, and Lippard, however, there is a tendency to abandon utterly traditional standards of "art"; while Dickens and Balzac were somehow having it both ways —triumphing in the market place, and yet preparing a place for themselves in the libraries and classrooms of the future. The radical popular writers, however, accommodated to the new possibilities and new audiences of their time in a fashion which won them the disfavor of the squeamish and genteel generations which immediately succeeded them, but which begins to seem to us now, in another antigenteel time, at a second stage of the Pop Revolution, immensely suggestive and admirable.

As in our era, so in the time of Lippard it was new technology which determined the new aesthetics; and, indeed, this is the essential nature of Pop Art. Certain technological advances had, in any event, made possible the printing of books at a price much lower than anybody had hitherto envisaged: the new rotary steam press; a new method of making paper, first introduced into England by John Gamble in 1801, but resisted by the industry until around 1820; the perfection of the stereotype, making possible quick reprintings; and, finally, the commercial development of lithography by the German émigré Rudolph Ackermann, who also persuaded the great caricaturists of the era to become illustrators. Those inventions were intended chiefly to facilitate the publication of popular newspapers, but they served also to bring about a marriage of journalism and fiction, creating that odd hybrid, the newspaper serial. And, indeed, the cheap novel, the "penny dreadful," *is* the newspaper novel: stereotyped on newsprint, copiously illustrated and appearing in weekly or monthly penny installments—the author never more than a chapter or two ahead of his readers.

Technology, however, could only make possible mass production of fiction; mass distribution depending ultimately on the creation of a mass audience, and this was the work not of engineers but missionaries. The spread of literacy in the time of Lippard was carried on chiefly in institutions established by the evangelical churches and various philanthropic organizations dedicated to the "cultural enrichment" of the laborer: Charity Schools, Sunday Schools, Mechanics Institutes. Once readers were present in large numbers and the price of books had been brought within their reach, the ingenuity of the businessman (particularly in England) soon created new ways of getting books into more and more hands.

In the age of Lippard and Reynolds and Sue, this meant the circulating library, as it had since the eighteenth century; and especially the railway-station bookstall, which was new. The stagecoach had proved a notably inappropriate mode of conveyance for reading, combining a maximum of disruptive motion with a minimum of light; but the railway carriage provided lighting conditions which made it quite possible to read, as well as a kind of comfort which bred that traveler's ennui which makes *not* reading almost impossible. The period, therefore, saw the emergence of a new view of reading, still alive in our time, as the form of relaxation or escape most appropriate to the trip into the country, or the start of a holiday, as well as to that happy state between waking and sleeping induced by the motion of trains.

The use of movies and stereo music on transcontinental and transoceanic air flights perhaps marks the beginning of the end of this period, but bookstands remain to this very moment a conspicuous adornment of all depots and airports. And the same sort of people still line up before them, as departure time approaches, grabbing a handful of books which must be cheap enough to be thrown away or left behind, and which must guarantee somehow total irresponsibility. Such readers, to be sure, are now—as they were then—not typically workingmen at all, but middle-class people, even students, slumming as it were: temporarily taking a holiday from the "serious literature" on their library shelves at home. Yet a large part of the readership of Sue and Reynolds and Lippard must have been drawn from this class—out of which, indeed, came those critics who in middle age disavowed what in their youth they had enjoyed, though even then (they were to claim at least) only as an unworthy indulgence, a minor vice.

It was not, however, primarily to or for such readers that Lippard and his colleagues wrote. He may have managed to earn between three and four thousand dollars a year with their help, but his books (like Sue's or Reynolds') do not represent a purely commercial response to opportunities opened up by advances in technology and new developments in bookselling; they are also, in a deeper sense, "popular," which is to say, aimed at educating the working-class elements of their audience to live better lives and even to make for themselves a better world. Lippard lived through difficult times as a youth, but is not himself of working-class origin, any more than were Sue and Reynolds and Gerstäcker; yet he was a convinced socialist, and, like his contemporaries, got into trouble because of his political activism. It must be understood, however, that his revolutionary doctrine was pre-Communist Manifesto socialism: not the "scientific" theory developed, with appropriate statistics and "laws," by Marx and his followers; but the sort of utopian, idealistic, sentimental dream expressed, with appropriate rhetoric and poetry, by Fourier and others, only to be mocked and belittled by Marx.

Yet whatever the lack in precision and sophistication of its social doctrine, the 1840s were a period at least in which for the first time it had become possible to speak of a "working class" rather than of "the lower orders" or "the poor"; and in which, therefore, it was also possible to imagine a kind of literature appropriate to a group thus redefined. Condescension had not disappeared entirely with the invention of a new nomenclature (any more than it disappears entirely among us now that we have learned to say "Black" rather than "darky" or "colored man" or "Negro"), since men like Sue and Reynolds were quite remote from their readers in social origin. Yet, unlike the kind of literature written at "the lower orders" and "the poor," fiction for the "working class" was relatively free of advice to its audience to know their places and accept their lot. Rather it held out to them the possibility of imagining (perhaps someday creating) a world in which they would fare better; or at least one in which the corruption of their masters would be exposed to scorn.

Quite obviously, the "penny dreadful" did not operate to change the visible world, as did, for instance, the revolutionary pamphlets and books of Marx and Engels; and yet it changed hearts and minds, altered both the self-consciousness of the workers and the consciousness of them among the bourgeoisie. Thinking of something like this, George Bernard Shaw, himself a life-long socialist, was once moved to remark that Dickens' *Little Dorrit* was a more revolutionary book than Marx's *Das Kapital*. And surely, even more directly and crudely than Dickens, Sue and Reynolds and Lippard used their kind of fiction to demythologize the upper classes and to mythologize the lower ones, to expose and debunk aristocratic life and to sentimentalize and glorify the life of the humble.

And precisely because it was addressed not to the reason but to the sensibilities of its readers, this fiction could not afford to be merely didactic or tendentious but aimed above all at telling stories of breathless suspense, creating vivid images of horror and lust, thus rousing passion and releasing it, over and over in a series of orgasmic explosions. The development of this sort of fiction is not linear like conventional plotting, but up and down, from peak to valley, tumescence to detumescence and back.

"Excitement" rather than "instruction and delight" is the end sought by the writers of the popular literature of the 1840's; and in quest of it they exploited, with the virtuosity of old pros, two basic human responses: sex and aggression. Theirs was, that is to say, a kind of fiction thoroughly sado-masochistic and at least demipornographic, though always in terms more political than domestic, more public than private. The brothel and the gallows were their preferred scene—areas where commerce and sex, law and violence oddly consorted. And this concern with public issues constitutes a bid for respectability of a sort.

Such pious and sado-masochistic subpornography must, therefore, be seen as occupying an unsuspected middle ground between that pre-empted by the novels intended for the "proper Victorians" and that exploited by those writers whom Stephen Marcus has called the "other Victorians." Unlike the pure Porn provided by the latter, political demiporn contains no crudely explicit language, no forbidden words, no actual descriptions of the sexual encounter, only a constant teasing of the imagination, a constant invitation to finish for one's self scenes which fade out in a swoon and discreet silence. We are often invited into ladies' beds or permitted to peep into their boudoirs, but never permitted to remain to the point of penetration of their lovely flesh.

And though there is some exploitation of female nudity, both in the text and the accompanying illustrations, to feed the erotic fantasies so essential to popular fiction, such nakedness extends only to the navel. There is typically—usually in the course of a lingering description of a disrobing as a prelude to seduction or rape—considerable exposure of what such writers are fond of calling "snowy globes," though of nothing below the waist. And, indeed, there is no more breast-centered concern with the female form anywhere in world art, with the possible exception of the Fountains of Rome and the center fold-out of *Playboy*.

It should be clear that the literature of the 1840's is a specific subgenre of popular literature—not merely produced by men only but intended for an exclusively male audience. It was, therefore, doomed to a temporary eclipse at least, not only by the more ambitious literature contemporary with it, the work of, say, Balzac and Dickens—but also by the pop literature which immediately succeeded it: those genteel best-sellers of the 1870's *(The Lamp-lighter,* parodied by Joyce in the Gertie MacDowell episode of *Ulysses* is an example) which represented an attempt to come to terms with the re-emergence of a bourgeois female audience—first appealed to by Richardson—as the controllers of the literary market-place.

In any case, it is the temporary dissolution of a politically minded male audience with a taste for subpornography, in favor of the domestically oriented female audience with a taste for pure sentimentality which explains the loss of approval suffered by Lippard's kind of fiction. And when that male audience reasserted itself at the very end of the nineteenth century and the beginning of ours, it had grown somehow less political, was willing at any rate to satisfy itself with the exotic adventure story, the detective novel and the Western—each projecting in its way a nostalgic dream of innocence rather than fantasies of exposure and revolution and sex.

The later pop forms for men only tend, in fact, to be tales of men only; but in the 1840's no male best-seller was without its female victims, raped or seduced by the evil rich, rescued and redeemed by the worthy poor—or more usually, by renegade aristocratic champions of the poor. Descriptions of the female form were as essential to the genre as they were to the sentimental literature read by the wives, mothers, and sisters of its fans. Yet how different those descriptions, in direct response to the differences of the fantasies which fed them and were in turn fed by them.

Here, for instance, are two contrasting passages, the first from the *Family Herald* of 1850, the second from Reynolds' *Wagner: the Wehr-Wolf.* They are quoted side by side in a study by Margaret Dalziel called *Popular Fiction 100 Years Ago,* presumably to illustrate Reynolds' superior skill and candor as compared to other contemporary mass entertainers; but they illustrate rather the diversity of the images of woman demanded, on the one hand, by the female popular audience and, on the other, by the male.

> Alice was one of those tall, aristocratic-looking creatures, who notwithstanding a certain slimness, realise, perhaps, the highest ideal of female beauty. Her figure was of the lordly Norman type, and perfect in its proportions; while every movement was grace-

ful, yet dignified. Her face was of that almost divine beauty we see in the Beatrice Cenci of Guido. The same dazzling complexion, the same blue eyes, the same golden hair. . . . Her countenance, always lovely, was now transcendently beautiful, for it glowed with enthusiasm.

She was attired in deep black; her luxuriant raven hair, no longer depending in shining curls, was gathered up in massy bands at the sides, and in a knot behind, whence hung a rich veil that *meandered over her body's splendidly symmetrical length of limb in such a manner as to aid her attire in shaping rather than hiding the contours of that matchless form.* The voluptuous development of her bust was shrouded, not concealed, by the stomacher of black velvet which she wore, and which set off in strong relief the dazzling whiteness of her neck.

And now Lippard in a similar vein:

Her head deep sunken in a downy pillow, a beautiful woman lay wrapt in slumber. By the manner in which the silken folds of the coverlid were disposed, you might see that her form was full, large and voluptuous. Thick masses of jet-black hair fell, glossy and luxuriant, over her round neck and along her uncovered bosom, which swelling with the full ripeness of womanhood, rose gently in the light. . . . And over that full bosom, which rose and fell with the gentle impulse of slumber, over that womanly bosom, which should have been the home of pure thoughts and wifely affections, was laid a small and swarthy hand, whose fingers, heavy with rings, pressed against the ivory skin, all streaked with veins of delicate azure, and clung twiningly among the dark tresses that hung drooping over the breast, as its globes rose heaving into view, like worlds of purity and womanhood.

Even from so scant a sampling it should be clear that the popular male novel of the 1840's is distinguished not only by a common subject matter and a shared stock of imagery, but also by a special style, which, invented in French, manages to survive in German, as well as in both British and American English. That style tends toward the breathless, the ecstatic, the rhapsodic, as is appropriate to a kind of prose in which the cadences of emotion are always threatening to break through the limits of syntax. And in some of the writers of the school, conventional marks of punctuation give way to dashes or dots to indicate the replacement of logic by passion, as in Reynolds, for instance.

> Even while he reflected upon other things—amidst the perils which enveloped his career, and the reminiscences of the dread deeds of which he had been guilty,—amongst the reasons which he had assembled together to convince himself that the hideous countenances at the gate did not exist in reality,—there was one idea—unmixed—definite—standing boldly out from the rest in his imagination,—*that he might be left to die of starvation!*

Sometimes the full stop is replaced not by the dash but by the exclamation point, or even double exclamation points, while paragraphs shrink to the single exclamatory sentence, as in Reynolds once more:

> A week contains a hundred and sixty-eight hours.
> And he worked a hundred and nineteen hours each week!
> And he earned eight shillings!!
> A decimal more than three farthings an hour!!!

The intent is clear, in any case: to write "badly" at all costs, which is to say, to choose an air of slapdash carelessness over any pretense at polish; to prefer clichés to well-turned phrases; and to let grammar take care of itself. Squeamish critics, both then and now, have tended to be put off by this affectation of banality and subliteracy, which is in fact, somehow functional and effective. I myself, writing about Lippard earlier[2], have fallen into that trap—betraying my own genuine fondness for his mad book by condescension, and thus revealing the "double standard" toward High

---

[2] In *Love and Death in the American Novel* (1960), where along with many observations which seem to me valid still, I felt obliged to talk about "a slapdash literary level considerably below that of his predecessor . . .," "shamefully masturbating dreams," etc. But throughout that study, it seems to me now, I tried to justify my quite valid determination to deal with "pop books" as well as "classics" with snide or ironical asides. It is one of the few things I would now change if I could without falsifying my earlier version.

and Pop Art which I find difficult to transcend. And yet reading in other critics such typical ploys as, "One cannot condemn Elvis Presley for not being like Gigli. On the other hand it is not enough . . ." or "One can study pornography by its own standards, but one has always to make it clear ˙. ." I know the limitations of such a double view, shudder to think how strongly and for how long it affected my own criticism.

In both realms of art, if in fact they are two, form follows function as it properly should. The structure of the subpornographic novel, for instance, is as unorthodox as its sentences, since—like many pop genres, e.g., the daytime radio and television serial—it tends to be all middle, with no real beginning or conclusion. The books of Lippard and Sue and Reynolds are, in essence, endless books. *The Quaker City,* though itself a fairly thick volume, is one of the smallest of the lot; seeming, indeed, almost slim for all its five-hundred-odd pages, when compared to Reynold's *Mysteries of the Court,* which ran to some four and a half million words, and Sue's *Mysteries of the People,* which covers two thousand years of history in enough pages to make perhaps fifty modern novels. What is reflected in their bulk is not so much the dream of writing the "total novel," a model of all human experience, like, say, Balzac or Faulkner, but rather the hope of entertaining forever an insomniac public quite as tyrannical as the story-loving Sultan of Scheherazade. The pop novel of Sue and Reynolds and Lippard represents, that is to say, a model not of swarming life but of the mass media themselves—an unremitting stream of words intended to combat a finally unmitigatable ennui.

Styleless and structureless, in any classic sense, the genre is also —and most disturbingly, perhaps—characterless. The multitude of persons who move through its pages are not portrayed in any kind of psychological depth; and certainly they never change, since they are representative rather than individual, *given* once and for all rather than developed in time. When such characters become memorable at all, it is as mythic figures, names of mysterious resonance inextricably associated with certain immutable qualities and postures; not as fictional personages, endowed with souls and lifestyles, pasts and futures. Moreover, as mythic figures they rapidly pass out of their inventor's hands into the public domain, where they are borrowed with no pangs of conscience by other writers, who sense, perhaps, that their presumed creators merely found them in the communal imagination.

The single book of Charles Dickens which belongs wholly to the popular genre is *The Pickwick Papers*[3]*;* and the archetypal character of Pickwick (suggested by an engraver to begin with) was appropriated by painters and potters and playmakers, as well as rival pop writers, in especial G. W. M. Reynolds, who sent him to France in *Pickwick Abroad,* gave him a wife in *Pickwick Married,* and actually turned him into a teetotaler in *Noctes Pickwickianae.* But why *not,* after all? Had not Dickens himself played a similar game, attempting to re-appropriate his own characters (quite as vainly as Shakespeare trying to revive Falstaff in *The Merry Wives of Windsor)* in *Master Humphrey's Clock?* Pop Art, even in the age of individualism, tended to be collective, collaborative—like the slowly accreting epics on one end of the time scale, and corporately produced movies on the other. Perhaps Sue and Lippard, maybe even Reynolds, may have regarded themselves on occasion as lonely artists trying to make a name as well as a fortune by their art. Typically, however, the author of this kind of fiction seems to think of himself as helping, along with his predecessors, contemporaries, and ghost writers, to compose an immense, cooperative, nearly anonymous work: a monstrous super novel, which exists not in the pages of any book with its author's name on the spine but in the heads and hearts of the mass audience.

Difficult as it has been for traditional criticism to come to terms with the antiform of the popular novel, it has been even harder for it to arrive at any final understanding of what its anti-ideas, which is to say, its nonphilosophical themes, really signify. There is, however, an essential clue to this in the word "mystery" or "mysteries," which appears in so many of the titles. As a matter of fact, even Lippard's book smuggles this key word into its second subtitle, "A Romance of Philadelphia Life, Mystery, and Crime"; and his German translator-adapter gave it an even more prominent place, calling his version *The Quaker City and Its Mysteries.*

---

[3] *Oliver Twist* and *Old Curiosity Shop* remain basically pop as well; but all of Dickens' novels after them aspire to become symbolist rather than mythological—tend, that is to say, toward "High Literature."

In recent times, the word has survived only in our habit of calling detective novels "mystery stories," as if the sole mystery in our existence was "Who done it?"; but this represents a reduced and demythicized use of a magic term with a long history. It is well to remember that it goes back, in fact, to the early days of the Gothic Romance, when Anne Radcliffe published *The Mysteries of Udolpho,* a classic example of the genre dedicated to evoking the darkness of medieval times. The mysteries of the 1840's, however, were concerned not with what was inscrutable and sinister in the outlived past, but what remained inscrutable and sinister in the living present; not with the darkness of the dungeons below medieval castles, but with the darkness of the urban underworld: all that lies beneath the glittering surfaces of the Big City.

Insofar as the subpornographic novel for males represents an attempt to redeem the modern city for the imagination, to invent a myth of the City as moving and mysterious as the ancient myths of Sea and Forest, it belongs to the mainstream of early "modernist" art; joining the "lowbrow" Sue and Reynolds not only to the ambiguously "middlebrow" Balzac and Dickens and Dostoevski, but also to such "highbrows" as Baudelaire and Whitman. The obsession with the infernal city suggests, moreover, a link between Lippard and Herman Melville; for the latter attempted at least twice (for London in *Redburn,* for New York in *Pierre)* the evocation of urban horror, calling on his memories of Dante, for whom "The City" had been a favorite metaphor for hell itself.

The concern with the city as landscape and symbol never quite dies out of "modernism" (think, for instance, of the "Unreal City" of Eliot's *The Waste Land);* but from the time of, say, Arnold Bennett to that of James T. Farrell, there was an attempt to demythify the City—to present it as banal, rather than horrific. To Lippard all cities may have seemed like Cities of the Plain ("Woe Unto Sodom!" cries the slogan on the title page of *The Monks of Monk Hall),* but to those who thought of themselves as "realists," such Biblical analogues came to appear merely sensational—and finally irrelevant. In pop culture, however, the image of the City as hidden horror never died, though it was driven underground—to Soho, the Bowery, the Tenderloin, into the aptly named "underworld" of the detective story and the thriller.

Then in our own century, it has begun to re-emerge—all the more terrifying because of its advanced technology—in Science Fiction: first, perhaps, in certain German films, in Fritz Lang's *Metropolis,* for instance; and next in comic books, whose versions of the Big City have fed the imagination of a generation of novelists and poets just now coming of age. Such writers have been especially impressed by the urban wilderness of Superman and Captain Marvel: that crime-ridden megalopolis—so conveniently supplied with phone booths for quick costume changes, and seen always from above—through which Siegel and Shuster's superhero has been pursuing his foes for a quarter of a century now; and that similar one—seen from below, from the abandoned subway tunnel (once more we are underground, which is to say, mythologically at home)—in which the newsboy Billy Batson, by saying the mysterious word "SHAZAM," becomes Captain Marvel.

But the task of mythologizing the threat of the City remains divided up in our world—a function shared by the movies, the co n ics, the novel. Reynolds and Lippard and Sue were moviemaker and cartoonists (with some aid from their illustrators) and makers of fiction in one, encyclopedic pop artists competing with no one except each other. Besides, the mythological city they evoked was still fully erotic, still *female,* as it were—neither desexed by technology, nor transformed by the skyscraper into an icon of a kind of permanent and sterile male tumescence endlessly repeated against the sky. Women could be had, if only in terror—raped, seduced, even killed in passion—in the mythic city of the 1840's; but in the comic-book metropolis of post-World War II, they could only be eternally fled in a general flight from passion. Sex, the female principle, persists only as the mechanical womb of the telephone booth or the subway, in which human flesh is converted into a kind of superplastic, invulnerable to bullets or love. No wonder that it was necessary to pretend that the pop-horror of the 1950's was intended for kids only![4]

---

[4] Interestingly enough, there has been an attempt in the dying 1960's to introduce sex—even pornography—into the comic books themselves; but this has so far been confined to certain "head" comics, produced for a special audience, the hippie community for whom Mr. Natural seems a more useful symbol than Captain Marvel himself or other more recent inventions for the mass audience like Sub-Mariner or The Hulk.

For the subpornographers of the 1840's, however, the essential image of the mystery under the city was the Gothic whorehouse: a hidden place where, among all the other commodities for sale in the great urban market places, daughters and sisters and wives are being offered to the purchaser rich enough to acquire them. Typically this place is disguised—as a fashionable milliner's shop in Reynolds, for instance—though it may simply be buried away out of sight, as in Lippard. In any event, it must finally be revealed, exposed—in an age where exploitation, social and sexual, is no longer blatant and open as in pre-Revolutionary days, but concealed behind the facade of "business as usual."

The classic Gothic Novel was radical in its politics, but radical in an oddly retrospective way; which is to say, its authors attacked the inherited evils of the past as represented especially by the Inquisition and the remnants of the feudal aristocracy. The writers of popular Gothic, on the other hand, fought against the new masters, not the old, the hidden rather than open exploiters: factory owners, capitalists, merchants, as well as the pimps and thugs who serve them, and the lawyers and clergy who provide them cover and camouflage. The popular novel thinks of itself, then, as exposing, revealing, muckraking; and in this sense, it is closely allied with the illustrated comic newspaper, which appeared just before it, to provide the "inside dope" on those in power—stripping the rich and beautiful naked to provide the impotent poor a kind of vicarious revenge, as well as a sexual *frisson*. Unlike such newspapers, however, the popular novel was aimed not merely at provoking a snigger and grin but a real shudder of horror as well, repulsion tempered with wonder and awe. The popular novel did not utterly reject the comic, but it yearned for the "marvelous," too. And here James Fenimore Cooper provided a more useful model than, say, *Figaro in London* or *Figaro in Sheffield* or *Figaro in Birmingham,* which were already being published in the early 1830's.

Cooper may seem, at first glance, an oddly inappropriate guide for writers about urban life; but there is, as those authors make sufficiently manifest, a sense in which the City can, indeed *must,* come to represent for modern man, as the Sea and Forest had for his ancestors, what remains hidden and uncontrollable in his own psyche, what survives in him of "The Wilderness": the primitive world out of which his waking self has emerged long since, but to which his dreaming self returns. Intending to build a shelter, a refuge against all that was savage and dark around him, man had (he discovered as the mid-nineteenth century approached) constructed in his cities only a new kind of jungle, a jungle of stone and glass, into which he ventured as into a strange land. Civilized man, which is to say, the literate European of the 1840's, felt first dismay at his alienation in the cities he had built, then excitement. If he was not at home in the urban landscape, he could visit there like a traveler, a tourist.

The popular novels of the 1840's are, then, like Cooper's, exotic novels, expressions of a kind of armchair tourism. And their exoticism had been made possible, even necessary, as a wider and wider gap had opened between the ordinary city dweller and, on the one hand, the Very Rich, on the other, the denizens of the urban underworld, who came, finally, to seem as remote and romantic as the savages of the American West: the real Apaches—as, in fact, the inhabitants of the Underworld of Paris actually were called.[5] Eugene Sue was aware of how much he owed to Cooper in his mythologizing of the urban wilderness; and it is instructive to read his own words on the subject:

> Everybody has read the admirable pages in which Cooper, the American Walter Scott, has traced the fierce customs of the savages; the picturesque and poetic language, the thousand ruses with the aid of which they kill or pursue their enemies.
>
> We are going to try to put before the eyes of our reader some episodes from the life of other barbarians, also outside of civilization, barbarians different from the savage tribes so well depicted by Cooper.
>
> Only the barbarians of whom we are speaking are in our very midst. We can brush against them if we adventure into the

---

[5] Romantic exoticism seeks to escape the tedium and alienation of bourgeois life by flight in four directions, Back, Out, In, and Down: backward in time like Sir Walter Scott; outward in space like Robert Louis Stevenson; inward toward the murky depths of the unconscious like Rimbaud; or down the social scale like Sue and, after him, the so-called "Naturalists." (It is interesting that Zola wrote one of the last "mysteries," *The Mysteries of Marseille*.) All forms of Romantic exoticism are kinds of vicarious tourism—the downward variety vicarious "slumming."

hideouts in which they live, where they gather to plot murder, theft; to share the spoils of their victims.

These men have customs of their own, women of their own, a language of their own—a mysterious language full of dark images and of bloody and disgusting metaphors.

How much better Sue understood the real meaning of Cooper, and, consequently, of popular literature than did Poe, who associated the appeal and limitations of both that novelist and his mode exclusively with the primitive setting. In a review of *Wyandotté* published in 1843 (when, in fact, Sue's *Mysteries of Paris* had already begun to appear serially, perhaps at the very moment that Sue was setting down his own response to Cooper), Poe wrote:

> . . . we mean to suggest that this theme—life in the Wilderness —is one of intrinsic and universal interest, appealing to the heart of man in all phases; a theme, like that of life upon the ocean, so unfailingly omniprevalent in its power of arresting and absorbing attention, that while success or popularity is, with such a subject, expected as a matter of course, a failure might be properly regarded as conclusive evidence of imbecility on the part of the author . . .

And he then adds, a little ruefully—though he had already tried his hand at both the sea-story and the Western in his single complete novel, *The Narrative of A. Gordon Pym* (1837–38), and the abortive *Journal of Julius Rodman* (1840)—that the themes of life on the ocean and in the wilderness were to be avoided at all costs by the "man of genius . . . more interested in fame than popularity."

It is an elitist declaration of faith, based on the conviction that of the "two great classes of fiction," the class represented by Cooper, "the popular division," is distinguished by the fact that its authors are inevitably "lost or forgotten; or remembered, if at all, with something very nearly akin to contempt." Yet though this may be true of George Lippard, it can hardly be said to be so of Eugène Sue—whose characters may be forgotten (who now remembers Rodolphe or Fleur-de-Marie?), but whose name has become, like Poe's own, almost a common noun; used sometimes, to be sure, with more than a touch of contempt and yet also of something else, something more.

At any rate, from the very beginning Sue thought of himself as of Cooper's party, rather than, like Poe, on the side of "Mr. Brockden Brown, Mr. John Neal, Mr. Simms, Mr. Hawthorne," writers of whom it can be said, still according to Poe, that "even when the works perish, the man survives." Long before he embarked on the *Mysteries of Paris,* he had, in fact, already written sea-stories modeled on Cooper's *The Pilot,* and had even received, at one point, a fan letter from "The American Walter Scott" himself, who was then voyaging in France. But Sue did not discover until he was well into his greatest book the sense in which he had managed to remain faithful still to his old master, still an exoticist and laureate of the primitive, though he had abandoned the ocean for the city.

Quite another model had been proposed to him by the friend who first suggested that Sue take up a brand-new subject matter, in order to reach "the people" and find "the future." Yet what exactly that new model was is hard to tell, though quite clearly it was English rather than American. Sue's latest biographer, Jean-Louis Bory, reports confusingly that "Gosselin brought to Sue an illustrated English publication, whose illustrations and text depicted the 'Mysteries' of London." The word "Mysteries" causes difficulties, setting the reader immediately to thinking of G. M. W. Reynolds; but the chronology is all wrong, backward—since it was Sue who inspired Reynolds, not vice versa. And, in the end, it seems probable that Gosselin's gift to his friend must have been Pierce Egan's *Life in London,* which appeared in 1821 with a dedication to George IV, the infamous "Georgie Porgie" who had kissed the girls and made 'em cry, while still the Prince Regent—with his plump popsie in Brighton and his mad father in London.

What an unlikely source Egan seems for a new literature aimed at what Gosselin described as "the world just ahead, the future, the people. . . ." His book, despite the feeblest pretense at moralizing, was in fact a tongue-in-cheek, satirical picture of young Oxonians lost in the midst of London's "sporty life": a kind of guide to "flash" debauchery. Its tone is indicated clearly enough by a prefixed song, also written by Egan, a kind of ballad to the first "swinging London":

> London Town's a dashing place,
> For everything that's going,

There's gig and fun in every face,
So natty and so knowing. . . .

Take your Daffy, All be Happy;
And then dash on, In the fashion,
Dancing singing full of glee,
O London London town for me. . . .

No "mysteries" here, certainly, or room for revolutionary fervor. And yet the clue must have been there somehow, somewhere, for an imagination trained by Cooper. Sue found it, perhaps, in the engravings by the Cruikshank brothers, those caricatures closer to the grotesque and more attuned to the terrors and wonders of "slumming" than anything in the bland text itself: in the plate, for instance, called "Lowest Life in London"—depicting with something nearer horror than farce "the unsophisticated Sons and Daughters of Nature at 'All Max' "; or in the almost queasy scene in which a spectacled voyeur at the harpsichord peeps over his shoulder at Jerry dancing with "Corinthian Kate," her breasts bared to the nipple. Even for the modern reader, Pierce Egan seems as often as not to be limping after his illustrator, to be, as it were, merely illustrating the illustrations, often lamely enough, when he is not simply writing captions. Certainly he views his own art in metaphors compulsively pictorial, as his chapter headings reveal from the start: "A Camera-Obscura View of the Metropolis, with the Light and Shade attached to 'seeing Life' "; "A Short Sketch of the Author's Talents in taking a Likeness . . . A Pen-and-Ink Drawing of Corinthian Tom."

It is more than mere accident that the popular novel of the 1840's begins with an author at a loss appropriating from sketches intended for someone else's work, someone else's quite different purposes, the images necessary to release his own deepest fantasy. A similar thing had already happened with Dickens, who had come upon Pickwick in an attempt to provide a text for certain sketches of "sporting life" already contracted for and delivered. But the novel only *finally* became pictorial, after having been first epistolary and dramatic. The first truly pop form of the Western world, it was invented over and over in its first two centuries of existence on the basis of models provided by other genres. Created by Samuel Richardson out of the letter book, it was re-created by Fielding on the basis of stage techniques and parody of epic, then recast by Scott on the pattern of Shakespeare become Closet Drama. Only in the forties was the last element added (we do not think of Richardson or Fielding or Scott, as we do, say, of Dickens as necessarily illustrated), opening a real link with the future (Gosselin was right, after all) not provided by the more traditional models of letter or drama. Once words are thought of, however provisionally, as secondary or subsidiary to pictures—or rather, cartoons—we are well on the way to comic books and Walt Disney, and the "silent film" that is to give a shape to the movies forever after.

Eugene Sue, however, seems to have had little or no sense of all this at first. The tone of Egan, as well as his resolutely *un*-mythicized versions of low life, began by merely disgusting him; and his initial response to Gosselin ran (we are dependent here on the professional liar, Alexander Dumas, but why not?): "My dear friend, I don't like what's filthy and smells bad." But his dear friend hastened to remind him that, as a doctor and descendant of doctors, he should surely understand that remedies for sickness are often found precisely by delving into "the stench and rot of corpses." Once into the stinking heart of the "mysteries," in any case, Sue seems to have forgotten his distaste for filth; or rather, discovered that he *liked* delving in it, found it, after all, *amusing. "C' est peut-être bête comme un chou. Cela m' a bien amusé à faire, mais cela amusera-t-il les autres à lire? Violà la douteux."* Stupid stuff, maybe, but it tickled me to do it. Will it tickle anyone else to read it, that's the question.

Real or pretended, Sue's final doubts proved as groundless as his initial ones, for his book was an immediate and spectacular success, hailed—despite a certain detached irony, an amused distance from "the people," which he maintained throughout—not only by bourgeois readers, but by "the people" themselves; and even by *La Phalange,* journal of the utopian socialist followers of Fourier. Professional critics, too, were overwhelmed, as were Sue's fellow novelists in Europe and America, delighted to have been given at last a model for democratizing the Gothic, politicalizing a literature of the Marvelous. Sue had finished the *Mysteries* in October of 1843; the dramatic version (which ran for seven hours!) was played to enthusiastic audiences in 1844; and in that very year Sue began his second dazzling success, *The Wandering Jew.*

It was an extraordinary year for the then New Literature, 1844: a year in which Balzac was publishing *Splendeurs et Misères des Courtisanes,* Dumas *The Three Musketeers* and the *Count of Monte Cristo,* and Dickens was finishing (his mind turned round by his first trip to America) *Martin Chuzzlewit.* Meanwhile Cooper himself, driven by the competition from England to sell his books at twenty-five cents a volume, was doing *Afloat and Ashore,* and Walt Whitman, grieving over the failure of his single novel, *Franklin Evans,* was secretly preparing to become a poet. It was, in short, a time of revolutionary beginnings and endings, of the exhaustion of old possibilities and the opening of new.

To the moment itself, however, it seemed chiefly the time of the triumph of Sue; and in a matter of months, the dramatic adaptations and adulatory reviews were followed by the imitations, as if to make clear forever (but how soon the records were to grow dim, the memory to be lost) that Sue had not merely written a best-seller, he had also invented a genre, infinitely adaptable wherever men lived in cities and longed to mythologize them. Paris itself occasioned an astonishing number: *The Mysteries of the Bastille, The True Mysteries of Paris, The Mysteries of Old Paris, The Mysteries of New Paris,* etc.; and the rest of the world hastened to enter the mythic circle: *Mysteries of Berlin, Mysteries of Munich, Mysteries of Brussels, Hungarian Mysteries*—and, of course, several *Mysteries of London,* including one by Paul Féval, who assumed for the purpose of writing it the "Anglo-Saxon" name of Sir Francis Trolopp.

Sue himself was to do a great deal more before his career was over, but nothing else which would stir the creative imagination of his time as his own had been stirred reading Pierce Egan, or rather looking at the caricatures of the Cruikshank brothers through the eyes of Fenimore Cooper. Even *The Wandering Jew,* despite its phenomenal success, represented in some sense a regression to earlier Gothic themes; the key figure of the Jew, for instance, came out of late medieval lore, and the obsessive concern with the threat of the Jesuits seemed something left over from the eighteenth century: *Ecrasez l' infame!* But the mode itself had been established once and for all, the mixture of gore and sex and socialism, sentimentality and sadism, eros and politics: a true literature of the world ahead, the people and the future.

The triumph of the reactionary forces in France sent Sue into exile after 1852, but it only confirmed his radical politics, and, indeed, made his late fiction increasingly didactic and doctrinaire. The incredibly long and pious *Mysteries of the People,* which traces the history of a working-class family from the time of the Druids to the verge of Sue's present, is the culmination of that trend—a homily in fictional form, translated into English appropriately enough by Daniel De Leon, whom Lenin once described as America's greatest socialist.

G. W. M. Reynolds was perhaps the most important writer to be influenced by Sue; but in a perverse way he seems to have followed his predecessor's path backward, beginning with imitations of the kind of neo-Gothic fiction suggested by *The Wandering Jew,* and only later writing books on the model of *The Mysteries of Paris.* One of Reynolds' first novels was called *The Mysteries of the Inquisition,* followed very shortly by *Faust,* and then by his earliest real success, a newspaper serial called *Wagner: The Wehr-Wolf.* That Sue was in Reynolds' head there is no doubt; for he had spent several years in Paris, where he had gone at the age of twenty-one to begin a new life with the twelve thousand pounds left to him at the death of his father. His parents had intended him for a career in the army, actually sending him to Sandhurst, but his commitment was to a life of journalism, and he invested his patrimony in a magazine, actually published in Paris, on which he employed Thackeray among others.

He was, in fact, the publisher-editor-chief-contributor of several magazines during his career, the most famous of which was called *Reynolds' Miscellany of Romance, General Interest, Science and Art.* In some ways his activities as a writer remained always subsidiary to his interests as an editor, or rather as a journalist-reformer intent on rescuing the working class from intellectual torpor as well as economic exploitation; and he therefore had no scruples about writing voluminously without reflection or revision—and even, on occasion, calling on the aid of ghost writers. Yet despite all of this, Reynolds was, in fact, a highly talented writer, unfortunately cast into the shadow by the immense presence of that contemporary genius, Charles Dickens. By a further ironical turn of the screw, however, it turned out to be the example of Dickens which inspired Reynolds, turning him from an initial interest in fantasy based on the past to a concern with the contemporary scene, especially with low life and the language appropriate to it.

Just as Sue had been triggered by reading Pierce Egan through the eyes of James Fenimore Cooper, Reynolds was awakened to his true vocation by reading Pickwick through the eyes of Sue. Reynolds' relationship with Dickens is not, finally, as one-sided as it may seem at first, since Dickens in the latter part of his career apparently learned a great deal from Sue, borrowing certain stereotypical characters and themes, even adapting certain incidents which struck his fancy. And at the very end of his life he was wrestling with a dark and difficult book, called (untypically for Dickens) *The Mystery of Edwin Drood,* which not only in its title pays a kind of homage to the tradition of the "Mysteries" brought to England by Reynolds.

Reynolds, however, is temperamentally altogether different from Dickens; for there is in him a certain element of Puritanism in regard to drink, quite opposite to the attitude which made Dickens almost Dionysiac in tone whenever he described men on the way to drunkenness. In an act of what seems deliberate blasphemy, Reynolds, in his first pseudocontinuation of the Pickwick series, turned Pickwick himself, that god of brandy and water (along with Sam Weller and his father), into a teetotaler; and then in another actually married him off—removing him from that blessed state of bachelorhood, that world exclusively male, in which drinking is a consummation as high and holy as sex in marriage.

Sex constitutes, in fact, the other major area of difference between Reynolds and Dickens; Dickens is notorious for his squeamishness in dealing with female sexuality, his resolve to keep his women, however passionate or theoretically depraved, fully clothed; whereas female nudity is for Reynolds a central image, almost an obsession.

Reynolds is a master of the strip tease, a near-genius at contriving occasions for disrobing his female characters, and for making the reader his accomplice in peeping at them through windows and keyholes and from behind curtains. There is, for instance, an extraordinary scene in his *Mysteries of London,* in which a handsome young preacher receives as a present from a lady parishioner a nude statue which turns out, in fact, to be that lady herself! But what Dickens and Reynolds do share, and what the native English tradition of "Newgate" literature—the celebration in verse and prose of criminals who came to a bad end—encourages in both of them, is an obsession with violence, especially as it is practiced by the law itself in the form of public executions. The sole form of explicit pornography which Dickens permits himself is horror pornography, the pornography of crime and punishment—Bill Sykes strangling Nancy, Fagin in his cell—and in this Reynolds is almost his equal; though Reynolds had some kinks of his own, including a fascination with body-snatching, the rape of the dead.

Reynolds had a long career as an exploiter of death and sex, and is the author of an almost incredible number of books, but the two which established his reputation as a popular entertainer *par excellence* and friend of the people are *The Mysteries of London* and *The Mysteries of the Court.* In a certain sense, *The Mysteries of the Court* represents a regression from his earlier work, a kind of retreat in time to the era of the Prince Regent, who was later to become George IV, and a shift in subject matter from low life to high life: from an attempt to portray the sufferings of the poor to a projection of fantasies about the corrupt pleasures of the rich. And it was this side of Reynolds which seems to have appealed especially to George Lippard, who, beginning his career younger than any of his contemporaries, had a larger store of dreams than of actual experience to draw on for the making of his fictions—dreams he had dreamed himself in loneliness and anguish, plus the dreams dreamed precisely for such alienated boys as himself by Reynolds, and, for that matter, Sue. Indeed, it is impossible to tell in Lippard's case, so single and communal is the tradition, which writer provided a form for his reverie; the Frenchman who had, in fact, appeared in American translation almost immediately, or the Englishman who had become a best-seller in the United States almost as quickly as in his own country.

We do know that in the case of Friedrich Gerstäcker, it was Lippard himself rather than either of his European predecessors who provided the model; though doubtless Gerstäcker's mind had already been prepared to embrace what Lippard was doing by the example of the other two. What Gerstäcker seems really to have wanted, however, and what only Lippard could provide, was the European tradition of the "Mysteries" rendered with an American accent; for Gerstäcker had made his career precisely as the expert on all that was exotic on the American scene. Most of his books, as a matter of fact, dealt with the American West in its wilder and more brutal aspects; and he survives to this day chiefly as a writer of boys' "Westerns," his books being continually republished in large print, with brightly illustrated editions, and garish covers showing sudden death among trappers and Indians.

He actually journeyed in the United States from 1837 to 1843, and his account of his experiences appeared in an English translation rather inaccurately titled *Wild Sports in the Far West*. In this account one finds, interestingly enough, no descriptions whatsoever of the kind of lynch-mob violence and banditry which he was later to describe in his best-selling *The Regulators in Arkansas* (1845) and *The River Pilots of the Mississippi* (1848). As a matter of fact, he seems to have spent his time when he was not hunting or sight-seeing at Niagara Falls, peacefully visiting settlements of fellow Germans, or baiting, like the good German he himself was, such occasional Jewish peddlers as he encountered. There are some literary references in his travel book about America to Cooper and to Dickens, quite as one would expect; but there is no mention at all of George Lippard whose *Quaker City* he doubtless acquired during his journey, and perhaps had already started to translate or adapt on his way back home. What Lippard's novel suggested to him was, quite obviously, an alternative form of New World exoticism, the evocation of the specifically American city—of Philadelphia, in fact, already associated in the European mind with that earlier American exotic, Benjamin Franklin.

But what *is* specifically American about Lippard's fiction? What, in fact, had he added to or subtracted from the already established European tradition in the book which Gerstäcker was to rename *The Mysteries of Philadelphia*? Most of what he provides is the standard fare for which the popular audience had already been prepared by Reynolds and Sue: much violence and much sex, plus

a good deal of socialist piety. Yet it has all been rendered in a setting at least theoretically different from London or Paris or, for
that matter, any European city; though Lippard's "Philadelphia"
seems most often to be located in a mapless universe of nightmares
rather than in the America of real geography.

Still we do hear on occasion voices undoubtedly American,
communicating not in Sue's argot or the "flash" slang of Reynolds'
underworld types—but in accents well on the way to becoming burlesque or vaudeville stereotypes, *American* burlesque or vaudeville stereotypes, "authentic" enough for a European ear like
Gerstäcker's at least. Here, for instance, is the "Devil-Bug," repre-
senting general American low life, in a style which seems a clumsy
foreshadowing of Huck's "Pap": "It don't skeer me, I tell ye!
. . . Ain't it an ugly corpse? Hey? A reel nasty Christian, I
tell ye! Jist look at the knees, drawed up to the chin, jist look at the
eyes, hanging out on the cheeks . . ." And here the equally evil
Negro Glow-worm, "the long rows of his teeth, bustling from his
thick lips": "Massa Gusty no want de critter to go out ob dis 'ere
door . . . 'spose de nigger no mash him head, *bad* . . . did you
ebber see dis chile knock an ox down. Hah-hah!" And, finally, for
the first time, perhaps, in American fiction, the Jewish accent of
Gabriel Van Gelt, "Ven te tings vos done, you vos to gif me ten
tousand tollars in goldt. Vot have you done? Left me to rots in dat
hole—viles you valksh on Cheshnut Streets? Got-tam!"

Aside from all this, what sets Lippard's book apart from those
on which he modeled it is a peculiar emphasis, somehow characteristic of America, on the sanctity, in a world otherwise profane, of
brother-sister relationships. Behind Sue's first venture into popular
fiction, there lurks a kind of family myth, too, but his involves a
father's long search for his lost daughter, whom he finally discovers
living as a whore; and whom he delivers—to the apparent satisfaction of European readers—from the brothel to a nunnery, from
utter corruption to total chastity. Lippard's fantasy, on the other
hand, imagines a brother in breathless quest of a sister whose virtue
is momentarily threatened: a brother who arrives too late to save
that sister's honor, but in time enough to kill her seducer, to whom
he is equivocally bound by affection from the start.

It is not merely the seduction of an unprotected poor girl by a privileged gentleman which furnishes Lippard with a key image for social injustice, but the setting of that act in an odd sort of ménage, which seems all siblings and no parents; reinterpreting seduction, as a matter of fact, as a kind of incest—the worst of threats to the integrity of the family. And in both of its aspects this refantasizing of seduction (long since given the status of a myth by Samuel Richardson and his first female imitators) is peculiarly American; since the obsession with brother-sister incest haunts the American novel from its beginnings in William Hill Brown's *Power of Sympathy,* through the early fiction of Hawthorne and Melville's almost incoherent *Pierre,* to that strangely but aptly titled book with which American "realism" begins, Theodore Dreiser's *Sister Carrie*—and finally to Faulkner's *Absalom! Absalom!*

Moreover, the impulse to understand social injustice not as an offense of person against person, or of society against the individual, but rather of the impious against the family, is also basically American. In *Uncle Tom's Cabin,* for instance, which appeared only a decade or so after *The Monks of Monk Hall,* Harriet Beecher Stowe attempted to convince her vast audience that slavery was wrong by portraying it as an offense against the sole institution presumably unquestioned by anyone, which is to say, the family once more. And doing so she helped release a flood of sentimental energy, which—joined to certain political and economic forces— changed a world by changing its mind, or rather its heart. Mrs. Stowe possessed, however, the power of making or evoking myths to a degree unapproached by Lippard; and, for better or worse, with Uncle Tom and Topsy she succeeded in mythicizing the Negro, as Lippard could not do at all with such comic-malign images of the Black Man as Glow-worm or his companion, Musquito. His true Negro, his absolute victim, was the seduced girl, *la traviata,* whom he more sentimentalized than mythicized, thus preparing the way not for a revolution, but only for more Pop Art—in fiction and drama and, especially, in song.

On the other hand, Lippard's book did produce social results in its own small way. The immediate occasion for *The Monks of Monk Hall* was an incident in which a Philadelphian who had killed the seducer of his sister was held for a while in a New Jersey prison, tried in a New Jersey court, and then, to the total satisfaction of his fellow citizens, acquitted by New Jersey justice. The popular acclaim which followed the release of the murderer led to the writing of Lippard's novel, which in turn helped create a wave of public opinion that resulted in the passage of an antiseduction law in the state of New York in 1849; though in the novel itself not the courts but a brother, taking the law into his own hands, revenges the wronged girl.

There is, in fact, something ambiguous, and yet once more peculiarly American, about Lippard's use of the seduction theme to justify the principle of vigilante justice, in the name of which the Ku Klux Klan would later be defended in the fiction of George Dixon and D. W. Griffith's film *The Birth of a Nation;* and as it had already been glorified in Gerstäcker's *Regulators of Arkansas.* "I determined to write a book," Lippard tells us, "founded upon the following idea: *That the seduction of a poor and innocent girl, is a deed altogether as criminal as murder . . . the assassin of chastity and maidenhood is worthy of death by the hands of any man, and in any place."* If the tone seems shriller than art or even rhetoric demands, this is surely because Lippard is ridden by an almost pathological obsession with the theme of a sexual assault against the sister; so that he is driven to identify at once with the seducer and the avenger—thus granting himself, as well as his reader, the double privilege of violating the incest taboo and inflicting punishment for such a violation.

His style, at any rate, in the passage toward the conclusion of the book in which he plunges into a kind of dithyrambic song of triumph, presumably sung by a murderer-brother over the fallen body of his sister's lover, reveals a passionate celebration of justified violence, inevitable, certainly, in any guilt-ridden mind; but perhaps essential as well to any revolutionary movement, and to the sort of literature which reflects and sustains its spirit. It is tempting to dismiss the writing as simply "bad," since Lippard lacks even the minimum amount of discretion and control which keep Reynolds and Sue just within the bounds of literary respectability. But everything that is "bad," i.e., indiscreet, vulgar, fulsome, about the following passage represents, at their most embarrassing, effects deliberately sought: the authentic music of the popular-erotic-sentimental-revolutionary novel, before "scientific" Marxism had taught socialists a rhetoric which separated them from the people and their preferred literature.

"Ha, ha!" the shout burst from his lips. "Here is blood warm, warm, aye warm and gushing! Is that the murmur of a brook, is that the whisper of a breeze, is that the song of a bird? No, no, but still it is music—that gushing of the Wronger's blood! Deeply wronged, Mary, deeply, darkly wronged! But finally avenged, Mary, aye to the last drop of his blood! Have you no music there, I would dance, yes, yes, I would dance over the corse! Ha, ha, ha! Not the sound of the organ, that is too dark and gloomy! But the drum, the trumpet, the chorus of a full band; fill heaven and earth with joy! For in sight of God and his angels, I would dance over the corse, while a wild song of joy, fills the heavens! A song—huzza—a song! And the chorus, mark ye how it swells! Huzza!

—1970

EIGHT

Chutzpah and *Pudeur*

IF *chutzpah* and *pudeur* seem an ill-assorted pair of words, one of those mixed marriages (or unblessed acts of miscegenation) which everyone thinks should not and cannot last, but everyone knows most often do, this is because they are in fact such a mismatch; which is to say, made not in heaven but in the head of some perverse matchmaker, some misguided *shadchan*—in this case, me. I had never seen them consorting together on a printed page, the delicate French word, appropriate to a tradition of tact and learning, and the vulgar Yiddish one, so suitable to a countertradition in which arrogance and self-deprecating irony reinforce rather than cancel each other out.

Yet why should they not lie side by side in cold print, I found myself thinking, since they already lived side by side not only in my own divided self, but also in the general culture around me—in American literature, surely, ever since Nathanael West, whose first book boldly displayed its affiliations with the most cryptic, i.e., *pudique,* of French schools, surrealism; and whose last shyly confessed its link with Jewish *chutzpah* by introducing an Indian, called only, in a bad Yiddish joke, "Chief Kiss-My-Towkus," meaning kiss my ass.

Not to have made the conjunction public, once it had occurred to me, would have been to betray a lack of gall, nerve, *chutzpah,* to put it precisely; but not to have regretted it a little almost immediately, would have been to reveal so total an absence of decorum that the very notion of boldness would have lost all meaning. In either event, I would have confessed myself half a man, half an artist, as these are defined in our oddly hybrid tradition, whose two poles Matthew Arnold (being an Englishman at home) termed quite catholically Hebraic and Hellenic, and Philip Rahv (being a recently arrived immigrant) renamed rather parochially Redskin and Paleface; but which I feel obliged to call (feeling neither just arrived nor quite at home) *chutzpah* and *pudeur*. It is not merely a matter of speaking in two tongues neither really mine, but also of insisting on a modicum of irony—that highest academic form of *pudeur*—and thus escaping from both the myth of Antiquity and that of the West, though risking, I suppose, a fall into the equally legendary present, into fashion rather than piety.

I am, at any rate, interested in exploring the basic polarity, as well as the basic ambivalence behind it, which this pair of words seems to me to define more suggestively than any other: a basic polarity in our very understanding of what constitutes art and literature. I am not meaning to suggest that the peculiar Western tradition of art is explained wholly or even chiefly by the tension between *chutzpah* and *pudeur*—merely that this tension plays a large part in determining our essential double view of what it is the artist says or does or makes. I have, as a matter of fact, reflected earlier on two other sets of polarities and ambivalences which also underlie our definition of art: Archetype and Signature in 1952, Mythos and Logos in 1958; and there is some continuity of a complementary if not a developmental kind between those earlier explorations, especially the first, and the present one.

This essay is, in intent, however, complete—not a total explanation but a self-sufficient one: the working out of an extended metaphor or conceit which, in theory at least, should provide a "model" for a large body of literature, otherwise difficult even to see wholly, much less to understand. Yet it is with some regret that I enter on this third (and, I promise myself, final) venture into literary theory. It is a literary form which I practice seldom and reluctantly, finding it a disconcertingly attenuated form of poetry, or more specifically, I guess, prose fiction, in which neither horror nor humor—two effects of which I am, perhaps inordinately, fond, seems quite suitable.

All forms of literary criticism I take to be art forms, but general or theoretical criticism is so genteel or super-*pudique* that it is driven to pretending it is science or philosophy—something else and presumably better, truer, more dependable. It is, however, the very shamefastness of literary theory, its love of disguise, which gives the game away; for, after all, the very essence of literature, or what at least we have agreed to call "literature" in the Western World, is a special use of words which sometimes alternately, sometimes simultaneously, reveals and conceals, exposes and hides: a dialectic movement back and forth between what threatens to become arrogant narcissism and what trembles on the verge of bashful dumbness.

This dialectic can be fruitfully discussed either historically or psychologically: either as it is recapitulated in the experience of the child or youth who begins to define his craft and the image of himself within our tradition, at first feeling, living rather than knowing that tradition; or else as it has been reflected in the long, slow evolution of that tradition itself, in terms, that is to say, of that tradition as it has come to be known. I intend, for reasons which I hope will become clear, to be chiefly historical in my approach, setting the problem in the context of what I take to be history, though others more positivist in their approach might prefer to call it myth or mytho-history: a particular version of the past best suited to illuminate what concerns me in the present.

I cannot, however, resist insisting to begin with on what most readers must already know—on the way in which, even at the earliest stages of his career, a nascent writer may well keep a secret journal, complete with lock and key; but which he ("she" is more apropos here, perhaps, since, mythologically speaking, *pudeur* is female) leaves lying about, unlocked, to be discovered by the first passer-by, even that ultimate invader of privacy, the parent. In a recent article on child poets, for instance, which appeared in *The New York Times,* the caption under a shy-proud ten-year-old face reads: "They don't know I write them"—and the reference of the pronouns is clear; the duplicity involved betrayed by the fact that the phrase was presumably spoken to a reporter and into a camera.

But it is not quite as simple even as that; for the young writer of the locked-unlocked, concealed-revealed journal will probably have developed a not-quite-legible hand, or a system of more or less deliberate misspellings to baffle his hoped-for discoverer. And at the next stage, the almost ultimate one (some writers, indeed, get no further ever), the still virginal artist will have invented for himself a special style, opaque, oblique, overgarrulous, underarticulate—somehow *diversionary* in any case—out of a shamefast desire not to be understood, not to be caught out, even if read! Think of those artists fixated on one or another of these deeply ambivalent, regressive styles: the reticence of Emily Dickinson, the endless qualifications of Henry James, the playful assault on syntax and punctuation of e. e. cummings.

But what exactly does the would-be artist play at concealing so transparently, and why? What, after all, did he produce long before he could muster words, which he was taught he must in all decency hide? What was he, in fact, applauded and praised for doing *out of sight?* The answer is obvious, and explains why so often the bashful beginning writer asked to show his work will answer, "Ah, it's all hogwash or crap or shit." The toilet is in our tradition, the prototype of the hideaway workshop, atelier, studio: the single habitually locked room in a house, where one performs in theoretical secrecy what "they" know in actuality he must be doing.

No wonder the most *pudique* and secretive writers are such palpable monsters of anality: Swift with his still secret "little language," and his obsession with excrement; Gerard Manley Hopkins with his poems tucked away, as it were, in his guilty asshole; Mark Twain with his hoard of shameful manuscripts concealed until after his death, and the give-away clue in his piece of privately circulated pornography, which begins with an attempt to conceal the real author of a fart and ends with an old man peeing away an erection. But the example of Twain's *1601* adds a disconcerting new factor, since the place of love is, he reminds us, quite as St. Augustine had earlier, *intra urinas et faeces.* Indeed, our earliest as well as our latest erections may be caused not by lust but by the simple need to urinate. The locked bathroom is, finally, also a spot for masturbation—for fantasies if not actual works of love, as well as for flushing away shameful wastes; and between its antiseptic white walls, two guilts are compounded into one beside the potentially symbolic roll of blank paper.

If anality signifies shame and implies concealment, orality, on the other hand, is a source of praise and a school for showing off.

The child is urged not to hide the first sounds he learns to make through his mouth, but to repeat them for an audience; and though he is quickly taught to excrete in private, his eating is a public performance. The high chair and the grownup's table are the prototypes, therefore, of the spotlight and the platform from which one recites, prototypes of publication.

How tempting in view of all this to make the easy Freudian identification of the artist's two conflicting impulses, *chutzpahdik* and *pudique,* with the mythological orifices on either end of the alimentary canal; to think of them as biologically, physiologically determined and therefore inevitable, universal. Such an identification would, however, profit by being itself exposed to history, examined in time; a process which might remind us that Freud's basic mythology of oral and anal was, as it were, toilet-trained into him: the product of a Middle European, bourgeois, Jewish mother, crying, as her descendants have ever since, "Eat! Eat! Talk! Talk! But, remember, keep clean, do it in the pot!"—with an implicit "for me, for your mama!" after each injunction.

It would be amusing, therefore, perhaps even instructive, to imagine the son of a non-Middle European, nonbourgeois, non-Jewish mother, who taught her child to eat in private lest he bring shame on her, and to do all his talking to himself behind lowered shades; and who further insisted that the best way of proving his love for her was to crap as frequently and copiously as possible—preferably in the presence of guests. "Fast! Fast!," such a mother might say, "but remember, too, bigger bowel movements or you'll break my heart!" A rather contradictory set of instructions, one must grant, but what mother was ever quite consistent or what mythology ever logical. And one can surmise, in any case, what different symbolic values our two alimentary openings would have, as well as how different "poets" and "artists" might be in such a world: professing macrobiotics, no doubt, indulging in milk shakes only in secret, but boasting to their proud mamas (laconically—or in gestures) how profligately they had spent their seed, and before how many bystanders they had produced record-breaking stools.

For me, in any event, psychological explanations tend to end in fantasies like these, once history has, as it must, broken in on their purity; and I propose, therefore, to start with a mytho-historical approach and let psychology break in only when it can no longer be resisted. Let us* begin then at the Beginning, with the more or less mythological assumption that at that primordial moment, before history existed at all, every song was sung and every story told in a single holy language, *lashon-ha-kodesh:* an esoteric tongue belonging to priests and shamans. At that point, there was not, in our sense, any "literature" at all, only "Scriptures," which is to say, "Revelation": something spoken through and, after a while, even written down by those priests and shamans. But writing itself was a further mystery—not a means of communication, but only another sign of the supernatural origin of what was revealed, one more warranty that in fact (i.e., in myth) it had come from the God or Goddess, Jehovah or the Muse: some supernal authority outside and before the human self.

Such a state, mythology tells us, could not long endure; since before history began, in order for history to begin, there was a Fall, the *Second* Fall according to the Hebrew tradition: a Fall which occurs not in the Garden of Nature, where man can only eat what is given him, not eat what is forbidden; but in the City, in the very midst of what men build with their hands, at the very height, in fact, of their presumably unlimited erection. Unlike the Fall in Eden, which is a fall from grace into morality, the Fall at the Tower of Babel is from the Tongue into many tongues, from "Revelation" to "literature."

From this point on, there exist for every would-be writer two languages: the Holy Language, which he may not even know but inevitably knows *about;* and the secular or vulgar language, his own "mother tongue," as we have come to call it. Thus history and "literature" are invented at the same time; since "literature" as opposed to "Scripture" is first spoken, then written (in a kind of unwitting parody of the sacred texts) in the *mammaloshen,* the *lingua materna.* This means that in a world divided rather than united by language, each man comes to speak for himself, and to others who always may not, frequently do not, really understand him. And it further implies that writing itself ceases to be a Revelation of a

---

* The canny reader will note that with this "us," my paper begins to move from the *chutzpahdik* first person to the *pudique* third—thus illustrating in its own form the thesis it is presenting—or rather, *I* am presenting.

single truth to all mankind, and becomes instead Confession-Communication of a personal vision to those few, if any, who will hear and comprehend.

No longer is it possible for the poet to pretend that he is a sort of divine ventriloquist's dummy or holy conduit. The very formulas with which he introduces his message are profoundly altered. Invocations to the Muse, where they persist at all, are felt as mere metaphors; nor does any manipulator of words dare assert, like his prelapsarian ancestors, "Thus sayeth the Lord," or "It is written." Instead, he is likely to stammer, "What I mean is. . . ," which amounts to little more than "What 'I' means is," or "What I mean am, what I am means. . .": a series threatening continually to end in the whimper: "That is not what I mean at all." The game of words, in short, is played now not in the light of eternity, but in the world of mortality, where the winner achieves not salvation but only fame. What is at issue when one claims to speak for God is life and death; while the confession that one speaks only for himself means that nothing but honor and shame are at stake.

Yet occasionally, even after the fall to literature and history, some blessed Bard (self-blessed, to be sure, but that is good enough) will arise, convinced that the Universe is infinitely hospitable, after all—at least to him—and he will cry his message loud and clear, as if Babel had never fallen and his own language were that spoken in Heaven. We know the names of those serenely *chutzpahdik* Bards, Dante and Shakespeare, for instance; and reading them, we are almost convinced that if not in the Empyrean itself, at least in the Earthly Paradise, the guardian angels converse in Italian or English. But most writers since the Fall have imagined themselves inhabitants of a Universe something less than friendly, a universe threatening at every turn to publish the news which they surmised from the start: that they are *rejected*. Think of the bugaboo of the young writer and all that is implied by its metaphorical name, the "rejection slip." No wonder most poets begin on guard, creating protections against being shamed, even as they invent strategies for winning recognition.

It may well be, as William Faulkner observed of Albert Camus in a moving little obituary, that no author since Babel has ever wanted to do anything more (or less) than to write on the fallen walls of the world, "I was here" and to sign his name. Certainly,

Milton suggested much the same thing in his own language, on a similar occasion: "Fame is the spur." But if *chutzpah,* in the seventeenth century or the twentieth, urges that the worst event of all is to die unknown, *pudeur,* at either point in time, answers that "Shame! Shame! Everybody knows your name!" is the most terrible of reproaches. And so the writer tries to have it both ways at once, *can* have it both ways at once, since all that we call literature was invented with this in view. He writes his name on the already scribbled wall, writes it large and dark to compel attention. But he encrypts it, encodes it—thus emulating those wily prototypes of the artist, Ulysses and Huck Finn, who never tell the truth right away: never begin by giving their right name, or telling the real story of where they have come from, whither they are tending.

Yet if poetry is, after all—as Dante himself confessed, for all his show of assurance—a *bella menzogna,* most beautiful of lies, then the true name of the poet is revealed precisely by giving a false one; since his most secret and authentic title is Liar, Deceiver, Man of Many Devices. He will begin with the joke of a pseudonym, inscribing: KILROY WAS HERE. MARK TWAIN WAS HERE. GEORGE ELIOT WAS HERE—meaning SOMEBODY ELSE WAS HERE. NOT ME. Or, as the shoddiest of all jests has it, "Boss, there's nobody in here but us chickens." At the end, however, he is likely to be joking more seriously, kidding on the square, as it were, by insisting in his last extremity (once more like the prototypical Ulysses) that he is really *OU TIS,* NOBODY AT ALL. *Pudeur,* in short, drives the writer first to plot disguises, and next to dream invisibility; so that he may be heard unseen and unscathed.

Not only Nathanael Hawthorne, then—as Poe once commented in an unfriendly review—but *all* writers—as Poe certainly should have understood—write in invisible ink, on occasion at least. And why not; since with one eye they tend to see themselves as spies, secret agents in a world so unremittingly hostile, that even, perhaps especially, at home they are in enemy territory. And so they feel compelled to communicate with their unknown compatriots (how can they ever be sure who they are, or even whether they exist?) in a secret language, in code.

For this reason, therefore, proper literary criticism, which is to say, the analysis of what is really new or forever inexhaustible in the realm of art, must be in large part cryptanalysis. Insofar as the artist is an agent, the critic must be a counteragent, engaged in a special brand of detective work made easy because the criminal he pursues has taken pains to leave clues everywhere. In fact, the artist is precisely the kind of outlaw or traitor who wants his crime to be found out: found finally not to be a crime at all; but only an act of supreme virtue, a true act of love, though committed with all the show of guilt proper to a crime. Sometimes that strange guilt for love is manifested in the sneaking shamefastness of *pudeur,* sometimes in the brazen arrogance of *chutzpah;* but it is all the same, for they represent finally not two impulses but one: a genuine ambivalence rooted in a single basic response.

Of what, then, does the artist perhaps not quite fear himself guilty, but surely fear he may seem guilty to others, so that in their presence, finally even alone, he is driven to cringe or swagger? If a crime at all or a sin, writing is essentially a lonely crime or sin, an offense without victims; and in this respect it oddly resembles masturbation—constituting a kind of reversed or mirror image of it, in fact. Like onanism, the creation of "literature" is an auto-erotic act, accompanied by, or rather creating, maintaining, certain fantasies. But in the realm of "literature" the auto-erotic act itself remains invisible, existing only in metaphor, by analogy; while the fantasies once they have been committed to writing, are quite visible, palpable, one is tempted to say, real. But this is, of course, quite the opposite of masturbation.

Even if we think of the act of writing as a kind of aggravated masturbation, which is to say, as exhibitionist auto-eroticism, practiced in the hope (and fear) of attracting an audience, which the writer hopes (and fears) will be stimulated to follow his example, the writer has displayed in public no living flesh of his own, only fantasies whose exposure is banned by no law of God or man. And should his act provoke widespread imitation, it would only make him a best-seller rather than a real seducer; since the masturbatory orgy set off by a work of art, however successful, is one in which no one assaults anybody but himself, and even that within the private chambers of his own head. Where then is the offense; and if any can be presumed to exist, who is the offended?

But once more we have been betrayed by analogy and introspection into the trap of fantastic psychologizing, from which only a return to history can deliver us. And, indeed, if the questions to which we have come can be answered at all, the answers must lie hidden in history itself: *real* history this time, which is to say, the actual records of the emergence of vernacular poetry in Provence toward the end of the eleventh century—the second beginning of "literature" in the Western world.

It is the essence of our culture that in it art was twice-born, poetry twice-invented, the first time in the Near East, the second in Southern France; and the living sense of that second time is preserved for us in the eleven surviving poems (one with its musical setting) by William, the ninth Duke of Aquitaine and the seventh Count of Poitou, sometimes known simply as William of Poitou. He was, his early biographer tells us, distinguished by his royal connections ("he had a daughter who was wife to King Henry of England, and mother of the young King . . .") and his skill at seduction ("he went about the world for a long time to deceive women . . ."). History remembers him, however, as one of the unquestioned firsts of literature: first vernacular poet of the modern world.

There is some indication, in fact, that certain traditions had already begun to gel before the time of William, though in poems which have not come down to us. But they could not have been long in existence, since the deep Middle Ages were hostile not only to the making of poems as such, but to any use of the vernacular in writing whose ends were not immediate and practical. Christianity had, as every schoolboy knows, begun by attacking the "literature" of Greco-Roman civilization—in part because it was hopelessly secular from the parochial point of view called in the Middle Ages "Catholic"; in larger part, perhaps, because its canon clearly constituted a kind of "Scriptures" for a rival, pagan faith. But the war of the church against, say, Ovid (who was bootlegged and preserved anyhow) was not so much a war against a poet or poets as one aimed at destroying the very concept of art which had sustained them.

The Saints who cried, "What has Athens to do with Jerusalem?" provided the ammunition for an onslaught against all culture after Babel, an attack on any kind of Confession-Communication opposed to a single Revelation. And the dream they inspired in the leaders of the Roman Church was a dream of a world reunified around a single canonical Book, *The Book,* as the Christian Scriptures were commonly called, translated into a single, universally understood tongue, i.e., a New Holy Language. Oddly enough from a mythological point of view, though understandably from the point of view of history, that language turned out to be neither Hebrew nor Aramaic nor Greek, in which the Old Testament and the New had originally been written, but Latin, through which the Caesars had tried to unify an empire. But to build with hands in history is to recreate Babel, and the Roman Catholic Tower of Babel, though presumably built on Rock rather than sand, fell like the Tower which was its prototype.

This time, however, the Confusion of Tongues occurred not in myth but in history, and its record can be read in letters and memorial inscriptions and casual graffiti. Not instantaneously as in legend, but slowly over the centuries, Latin became Italian and French and Provençal; so that finally even crying assent to the Christian God, the inhabitants of the old Roman realm heard themselves shouting out variously, *"Si"* and *"Oui"* and *"Oc."* Small wonder they chose to address, feeling free for the first time, those lesser divinities, the women they loved, in those same divided tongues. It was, in fact, in the *langue d'oc,* the language of Rome's First Province, that "literature" was reborn; and William, to whom it was not even really native, picks it up, his lines trembling still for the sensitive ear—not only with the shudder of passion released, but with an additional tremor of delight at exploiting precisely what was *not* a Holy Language—the first vulgar tongue in which it had become possible to say again the personal "I," to write again a signed poem.

Over and over, his poems begin with slight variations on the single formula: *I will make a poem, a verse, a little song*—as if he can never exhaust the wonder and newness of his enterprise: the "I" singing, after long silence, its own vision of the world in the *lingua materna.*

> Companho, faray un vers . . . convinen:
> Farai un vers de dreyt nien:
> Farai un vers, pos mi sonelh . . .
> Farai chansoneta nueva . . .

Four times he manages the formula in the first line, then once in the second:

> *Pos de chantar m'es pres talentz,*
> *Farai un vers, don sui dolenz:*

And the repetition conveys finally something more, something other than a sense of joy and release. *Grand seigneur* that he was, William, one suspects, must have been a little scared—aware of what was dangerous, or would be found so by the Church, in his unprecedented venture. Yet how could he have known what lay ahead, what he was releasing in his playful or melancholy comments on his adventures with women?

Perhaps it is only our retrospective knowledge of the terror and beauty which followed him in history—the scores of poets who followed his example and the repression which ensued—that leads us to read an undertone of bravado and terror into his verse. It was not, after all, the poetry of William or any other *jongleur* that cued the Albigensian Crusade, but profound doctrinal differences, a conflict of religions. And yet when the culture of Provence was destroyed by the armies of the Church, not only the alleged Manichaean faith of the *Cathari* went down with it, but also the cult of *Joia,* of sexual pleasure, to which Provençal poetry was dedicated. That kind of poetry moved elsewhere, to be sure—into the languages of *oui* and *si* first of all; but it had died forever in the lovely tongue William once chose as specially suited to his needs. *"Qu'eu non ai soing d'estraing lati,"* he had written long before the blow fell, *"Qu'e m parta de mon Bon Vezi."* "I need no stranger's tongue, no alien Latin, which might separate me from my Good Neighbor."

Even with a shift into *"estraing lati",* which is to say, foreign vernaculars, William's example continued to impose itself; for he had somehow hit upon two poetic modes whose uses and possibilities have not yet been exhausted. Neither an especially subtle thinker, nor a very sensitive lover, nor an extraordinarily gifted technician, he managed somehow to invent, re-invent, find in the *langue d'oc* two forms appropriate to the two poles of the ambivalence about making verses which was to trouble his successors, if it did not already trouble him: the Enigma to express *pudeur* (in the poem beginning *"Farai un vers de dreyt nien"),* the Pornographic Song to register *chutzpah* (in the one opening *"Farai un vers, pos mi sonelh").*

The Enigma or the Riddle is a genre which we are likely to associate these days solely with the nursery and the child's book, though it is closely related to an adult form much prized in recent decades—the Conceit, which is to say, the extended, farfetched metaphor as practiced pre-eminently by John Donne. If we had not been told, for instance, in the sixth stanza of the perhaps-too-often cited "A Valediction Forbidding Mourning" that the poet is describing "Our two souls . . . which are one"—and reminded again in the third line of the seventh—the pair of stanzas which follow would be a Riddle rather than a Conceit:

> If they be two, they are two so
>   As stiff twin compasses are two;
> . . . the fix'd foot, makes no show
>   To move, but doth, if th'other do.
>
> And though it in the centre sit,
>   Yet, when the other far doth roam,
> It leans, and hearkens after it,
>   And grows erect, as that comes home.

An Enigma is, in fact, nothing but a Conceit which conceals one pole of its similitude in its tail, instead of presenting it forthrightly at its head. Moreover, even as the Conceit tends to become the Enigma, which, in a sense, it was in the beginning; the Enigma aspires to become—teases us with the possibility, even occasionally succeeds in becoming—the meta-Enigma, or Ultimate Riddle, fit symbol of the mystery at the heart of our existence: the Question without an Answer. Surely many children, all children, perhaps, must feel (as I myself once did) that the "answers" to certain well-loved riddles are irrelevant, a delusion and disappointment, a grown-up hoax intended to persuade them of what they instinctively know to be untrue: *that there is an answer to everything* and that it is the function of language to reveal that answer in story and song.

No wonder the wise child loves so desperately, before he realizes quite why, such anti-Riddles as Lewis Carroll's "Why is a raven like a writing desk?", to which the proper response is silence, or even better, laughter. Wonderland is, indeed, the school in which he learns to respond for ever after to the meta-Enigma, whether proposed jocosely, as in *Finnegans Wake,* in the form of a dreamed pun, "Why do am I look alike two poss of porter pease?"; or proffered quite seriously, as at the opening of Thoreau's *Walden,* in the guise of a confession or anticonfession:

> I long ago lost a hound, a bay horse, and a turtledove, and am still on their trail. Many are the travelers I have spoken to concerning them, describing their tracks and what calls they answered to. I have met one or two who have heard the hound, and the tramp of the horse, and even seen the dove disappear behind a cloud, and they seemed as anxious to recover them as if they had lost them themselves.

In Thoreau the question mark by which we are accustomed to identify the Riddle has been ingested, as it were; and we are confronted not with the puzzle itself but with a narrative about puzzle-asking ("I have spoken . . . describing their tracks . . .") and the bafflement of those asked. And we are here very close to what is generally called—once more with connotations of the nursery—Nonsense, i.e., the unanswerable Riddle without even a mark of interrogation to tease us into believing that there are answers at the back of *somebody's* book.

Nonsense always trembles on the verge of the ridiculous, though sometimes its practitioners seem blessedly unaware of the fact, as was Edgar Allan Poe, along with his French translators and imitators, Baudelaire and Mallarmé. A case in point is the following excerpt from *Ulalume:*

> These were days when my heart was volcanic
> As the scoriac rivers that roll—
> As the lavas that restlessly roll
> Their sulphurous currents down Yaanek,
> In the ultimate climes of the Pole—
> That groan as they roll down Mount Yaanek,
> In the realms of the Boreal Pole.

And for those still unaware of how funny the last two lines are, a reading of the notes in a recent scholarly edition (explaining the "Boreal Pole" is *really* the South Pole; and "Yaanek" a name derived either from "an Arabic execration, . . . probably obscene" or a term "sometimes used by Polish Jews for an unkindly Christian.") will perhaps suffice to illustrate at least the joke of seriously trying to solve Nonsense, or even Non-Sense, no matter how grave its tone. But Edward Lear—whom W. H. Auden has described as Poe's sole real imitator *in English*—guessed the secret long before us, revealing it in poems clearly intended as comic Nonsense (as opposed to mantic Non-Sense), though echoing Poe in cadence and sound pattern and especially in the invention of exotic-ridiculous place names.

> And in twenty years they all came back,
>   In twenty years or more.
> And every one said, 'How tall they've grown!
> For they've been to the Lakes, and the Torrible Zone,
>   And the hills of the Chankly Bore';
> And they drank their health, and gave them a feast
> Of dumplings made of beautiful yeast;
> And everyone said, 'If we only live,
> We too will go to sea in a Sieve,—
>   To the hills of the Chankly Bore!'

But what a crew they are, after all, these not-quite-askers of insoluble riddles; what guilt-ridden evaders of the public eye, what deviously invisible or masked men: Lewis Carroll and Henry David Thoreau, Edgar Allan Poe and Edward Lear. What artful dodgers into the nursery or the Azure—where fantasies of pederasty or necrophilia or incest, of sexual transgressions dreamed rather than dared are barely glimpsed past the concealing devices suggested by extreme *pudeur*. Not much doubt remains in their cases, that the Enigma is the form to which a writer turns when his awareness of guilt inclines him toward the pole of *pudeur;* when he lays, as it were, his finger to his lips or sticks his thumb in his mouth, thus betraying what he cannot, will not confess: *"I am guilty as hell, but no one knows it or ever will;* for how can they suspect, accuse, convict an Angel in Exile, or a mere child in adult form, of ultimate iniquity.

> *I* was a child and *she* was a child,
>   In this kingdom by the sea;
>   But we loved with a love that was more than love—
>   I and my Annabel Lee—

Finally, however, precisely the pretense that the Riddle is a child's game gives away the sexual secret it tries to conceal; verifying what we learn from other sources: that everywhere in mythology, the Enigma is associated with the threat of incest—as Claude Lévi-Strauss reminds us in a remarkable passage of his inaugural address at the Collège de France. "Between the puzzle solution and incest there exists a relation," he writes, "not external and of fact, but internal and of reason. . . . Like the solved puzzle, incest brings together elements doomed to remain separate. . . ." And he then goes on to explain that "the audacious union of masked words or of consanguines unknown to themselves . . . engenders decay and fermentation, the unchaining of natural forces . . ."; and therefore brings on "an eternal summer . . . licentious to the point of corruption," yet often chosen in history and myth over "a winter just as eternal . . . pure to the point of sterility. . . ."

The unsolved and insoluble Enigma, the Non-Sense Riddle, for which William provided the prototype, is quite another matter, however; since it represents averted rather than achieved incest, guilt without consummation. William's model opens, as a matter of fact, with a disavowal of all guilt, a disavowal of everything; but the order of that everything amounts to a backhand confession.

> *Farai un vers de dreyt nien:*
> *Non er di mi ni d'autra gen,*
> *Non er d'amor ni de joven,*
>   *Ni de ren au . . .*

"I will make a poem of pure nothing," he begins; and we are reminded, a little absurdly, of the adolescent's answer in the old joke: "Where are you going?" "Out." "What are you doing?" "Nothing."

But then he starts to specify, "It is not about me or anybody else; it is not about love or youth, or anything else." "*I* will make a poem," the boastful formula asserts; but by the second line the singer has begun to deny his singing self, the "I" released by the vernacular tradition. First the self, and then love and youth; these are the foci of his guilt—and what therefore his poem must aver is *not* his subject, though it cannot help naming them. And who can blame him, in any case, for what floats to the surface of his mind, since he has dreamed it all (he hastens to assure us next) "asleep and on horseback."

> *Qu'enans fo trobatz en durmen*
> *Sobre chevau.*

Why then is he trembling at the point of death a couple of stanzas later, afflicted by a malady of which he knows only "what they tell me"?

> *Malautz suy e tremi murir,*
> *E ren no•n sai mas quan n'aug dir . .*

He may assure us over and over that he couldn't care less about whatever is really at stake behind all his mystification ("I prize it no more than a mouse . . . I esteem it no more than a cock . . ."), but the note of melancholy and terror will not be exorcised; the counterpoint of *timor mortis conturbat me*. And lest we have forgotten, or never quite realized, that it is a Riddle we have been presented, the final line teases us with the hope of a solution, a key, *"la contraclau,"* that can only be provided by another, answering poem. *Fag ai lo vers,* the poet has assured us only five lines earlier, "and now my story is done." But, of course, it is not—since the meta-Enigma, the Riddle Without an Answer, is in essence endless, a tale without a conclusion.

"Every telling has a tailing," James Joyce was to insist more than eight centuries later, "and that's the he and she of it." But the Absolute Riddle has precisely no "tailing" *("Non er d'amor ni de joven"),* no "audacious union of . . . consanguines . . ."; and without consummation there is no conclusion. The unsolved puzzle like the taboo mother is Ever Virgin, never quite possessed. William, however, wrote not only of love as forbidden and therefore repressed, but also of passion as forbidden yet irrepressible—providing a prototype for the poetry of *chutzpah* even as he had for that of *pudeur.*

That other prototype, however, turns out to be quite simply the pornographic poem: the vaunt of potency, the boast of full genitality —delivered not from the crouch of shame with the finger to the lips, but with a sexual swagger, the hips thrust forward and the arms spread wide for an embrace. Whenever poetry, in fact, becomes *chutzpahdik* rather than *pudique,* in Walt Whitman, say, or Allen Ginsberg, it learns again to talk dirty. Before the arrogant poet can be loved he must first be condemned as "the dirtiest beast of the age," then, not cleared of that charge but found through it, loved for it, quite as in the case of Whitman. The shamefast poet, on the other hand, must first be blamed for his *obscurity,* then without being absolved, found through it and loved for it, quite like Gerard Manley Hopkins. Whitman and Hopkins—they seem ideal, almost allegorical opposites; and yet as Hopkins himself was driven to confess (shyly, his finger characteristically to his lips): "I always knew in my heart Walt Whitman's mind to be more like my own than any other man's living. . . ." It is as close to confessing the particular guilt that dogged him, the homosexuality he shared with Whitman, as Hopkins could come; but it is also a reminder of the sense in which *chutzpah* and *pudeur* are originally and finally one, two faces of a single ambivalence.

But William alone could suffice to remind us of this, since his most successful piece of pornography is about a *chutzpahdik* character (called once more quite simply "I") who managed by shamming the discretion of *pudeur* to achieve a kind of total sexual satisfaction: "Eight days or more" in a Provençal Pornotopia, with a pair of uninhibited women, who first feed him up on capons, white bread, good wine and "pepper in abundance," then almost screw him to death.

> *Tan las fotei com auzirets:*
> *Cen e quatre vint et ueit vetz,*
> *Q'a pauc no·i rompei mos corretz*
>   *E mos arnes,*
> *E no us puesc dir lo malaveg,*
>   *Tan gran m'en pres.*

"So much I fucked them," William sings, "as you shall hear: One hundred and eighty-eight times, so that I almost broke my braces and my straps; and I can't tell you what misery ensued, it was so great."*

In order, however, to attain that good, which, as he tells us in another poem, men desire more then all else in the world *("esta ben . . . D'acho don hom a plus talen"),* but which, as we learn from this one, can end in pain, the poet finds it necessary to simulate precisely the dumbness associated with *pudeur.* He is, in fact, the least faithful of all versifying lovers to the vow of secrecy theoretically essential to Courtly Love. Not only does he boast again and again in his *chutzpahdik* songs of his sexual prowess in general ("I've never had a lady at night who has not eagerly awakened me next morning. . . . I could have earned a living by my skill. . . ."), but he names names: denominating, for instance, the pair he fucked one hundred and eighty-eight times, first by their husbands' names, then by their Christian ones.

In the poem itself, however, he responds to their courteous-erotic greeting—delivered, as he puts it, in the vernacular of one of the ladies *("en son latin")*—in the nontongue of the deaf-mute: not *"but"* or *"bat"* but only *"Babariol, babariol, Babarian);* and says no more, though, to test him, they drag their long-clawed, vicious cat down his naked back. *"Babariol, babariol, Babarian,"* it is a nonsense poem, a riddling song—a way of saying nothing, of guaranteeing that he is constitutionally incapable of exposing what actual *chutzpah* lurks behind their superficial *pudeur.*

Once loose from the prison of their bedroom, however, the poet finds his shameless tongue; singing once more between waking and sleeping, though this time afoot and in the broad daylight, how lustful and wicked and guilty they were, women are—how sly and indefatigable and *innocent* he turned out to be, men always turn out to be. It is the typical stance of the *fabliaux,* not of the love songs of Provence with their pretense of male humility, their vows of discretion and silence; and suggests disconcertingly the sense in which much of that poetry might be, or at least can be, understood as

---

* In the standard scholarly text, *Les Chansons de Guillaume IX,* edited by Alfred Jeanroy, there is a running translation of the text into modern French, but this stanza is coyly represented (in a book revised in 1964!) by a row of dashes; nor does the verb *fotre* appear at all in the appended glossary—which is, I suppose, a case of academic *pudeur* at its most ignominious in vain combat with the artist's *chutzpah.*

mock-humble only, a strategy in the game of seduction. It is what comes of singing at the unguarded moment of falling asleep on the broad highway: "I will make a verse, since I am falling asleep, walking and taking the sun."

The poems of *chutzpah,* William's poetry suggests, are written on the verge of sleep, just as those of *pudeur* are composed in its very depths: the one in the reverie that prepares us for the fatal loss of consciousness, the other, at the moment when, disturbed, we must either dream or start awake. And how finally appealing they both are—the dirty story, so appropriate to the eternal adolescent in us, and the riddle, so suitable to the immortal child; the wet dream which we prepare for ourselves before we have quite lost consciousness, and the irrational sequence of the not-quite-nightmare, which our unconscious prepares for us to forestall a little the advent of guilt-ridden awareness; the fantasy of consummation without guilt, and its twinned opposite of guilt without consummation.

Neither, though, not even both together, served to keep William (representative in this respect of the Christian conscience of Europe) quite at peace, waking or sleeping. And he closes his career by inventing or perfecting a third prototype: the poem of recantation, which begins untypically: *"Pos de chantar m' es pres talentz"* —but in which the old formula *"farai un vers"* appears in the second line, this time qualified, however, with the word *dolenz,* sorrowful, mournful, melancholy. Yet even at this point, he cannot forgo a boast in retrospect, confessing—half ruefully, half proudly —even as he assures us that he wishes to surrender all for the sake of God and his own salvation, "I knew joy and pleasure, far and near and in my own domain." Nonetheless the recantation does in theory represent a disavowal of everything which the opening up of a vernacular, secular tradition had seemed to promise: a rejection of songs of joy in favor of songs of sorrow, of the celebration of self in favor of the denial of self, of poetry in favor of piety. But for piety, not the *"latin"* of Agnes, wife of *en* Guari, but that of the Church, which is to say, real rather than mock Latin is appropriate.

The tradition which William helped to inaugurate did not, however, disappear when he lost, or played at losing, his nerve. Men have, as every reader knows, continued to write in the *lingua ma-*

terna; and such writers, along with those readers, have tended ever since his time to divide their allegiances between his two proto-types. The majority have always preferred pornography, the poetry of sexual consummation and its celebration—though most often they have bowdlerized it, saying *amar* rather than *fotre,* out of re-spect for the *pudeur* of their lovers or their audiences or the official censors. But a considerable minority, all the way from the academy to the nursery, have opted for the Riddle—though this, also, has been bowdlerized, by those too proud or scared to confront the Total Enigma, the Question without any Answer at all.

Academics, especially, have proved *chutzpahdik* enough behind their masks of *pudeur* to prefer the quasi-Enigma, the Riddle insol-uble to the uninitiated many, yet decipherable by the tiny congrega-tion of the chosen: a symbol not of the opacity of all existence, but of the mystery of election. "Many are called but few are chosen," sing the poets of the quasi-Enigma; to which the quasipornog-raphers answer in chorus, "All the world loves a lover." And the Provencals had invented quite early names for both of these schools; calling the former *trobar clus,* which is to say, hermetic or private poetry, and the latter *trobar leu,* which means light or open verse.

Arnaut Daniel is the master of the *trobar clus,* "the greatest craftsman of *la lingua materna,"* according to Dante, who actually wrote eight verses in Provençal, the first of mother tongues and Daniel's own, to show his love for the earlier poet as well as the skill he thought he owed to his example. Moreover, Dante com-posed sestinas, too, imitating the difficult form Daniel had presuma-bly invented. Dante's grave and tormented poems, however, have little of the playfulness, the willingness to walk the brink of non-sense, which characterizes the Provençal poet, who set himself the task of ringing changes on the words for "fingernail" and "uncle" (in the *langue d'oc, "ongla"* and *"oncle,"* words which tease us with their closeness of sound, their dissonance of meaning) in his famous sestina; and whose boast was, in love as well as art, that he "yoked the ox and the hare" and "swam against the current."

What Dante did understand is that the poetry of *pudeur,* the true *trobar clus,* is no mere pastiche of rare words and rich rhymes but a kind of verse built to keep out rather than let in—a way of using words as if they were opaque: not as windows opening on the soul, but reflecting jewels which redouble whatever light we cast on them, and end by dazzling us, blinding us with their icy splendor. *Trobar clus* is the poetry of winter light and winter cold—celebrating, in fact, precisely that "winter just as eternal . . ." to which Lévi-Strauss alluded, "pure to the point of sterility. . . ." And this, too, Dante comprehended, beginning his own hermetic sestina:

> To small daylight and the great circle of shade
> I've come, alas, and to the blanching of the hills,
> The season when the color leaves the grass. . .

quite on the model of Arnaut Daniel, who opens one of his thorniest, most forbidding poems:

> The bitter air
> Makes branchy boughs
>   Quite bare
> That the sweet made thick with leaves. . . .

The poets of the *trobar leu,* on the other hand, of whom Bernart de Ventadorn is the most eminent and best remembered (nearly fifty of his poems have been preserved, as opposed to eighteen by Daniel), set their songs against a landscape not white but green, not chill but warm. Spring is their symbolic season:

> The sweet paschal season
> With its fresh greening
> Brings leaf and flower
> Of diverse color . . .

Their weather is not quite Lévi-Strauss's "eternal summer . . . licentious to the point of corruption," of which, in some ways, William's overheated interiors inhabited by overstuffed lovers—that world of glowing coals and plenteous hot pepper—seems a nearer analogue; and certainly when William does take us outdoors, it is into a sweet springtime appropriate to a poetry of unabashed sensuality: *la dolchor de temps novel,* in which trees burgeon and birds sing, as if an eternal summer lay just ahead. Springtime represents, perhaps, a compromise, a withdrawal to the moment of promised rather than accomplished bliss, on the part of poets more timid than William, but not less committed finally to the cult of *joia*. And even when they seem to celebrate an eternal April without a June, an eternally retreating horizon, at least it is a benign one. Not, in fact, until the time of T. S. Eliot does any poet portray April as more cruel than kind; since only the tradition of "modernism" and the *avant-garde* permits, as it were, the frozen winter of *trobar clus* to creep past the vernal equinox.

Yet the poetry of the Waste Land is not unprecedented in making the impossibility of love its central subject, innocence as a function of impotence its second theme. Nor is it different from the main stream of *pudique* verse in its resolve to be deliberately "difficult" or "obscure," i.e., in determining to encode its secrets in a language comprehensible only to those already in the know. What is new is the particular language it employs—that blend of allusion and demiquotation in a Babel of tongues, which represents at once the climax and dissolution of a linguistic experiment carried on ever since the Renaissance: the attempt to create a "glorified" or "illustrated" vernacular, a proper "poetic diction," different, on the one hand, from the Christian Holy Language, which was Latin, and, on the other, from the simple prattle of women and children. It was certain insecure academics who had learned to be ashamed of not speaking the languages of Classical Antiquity, and therefore speculated on the possibility of creating a kind of half-holy tongue by splitting their own *lingua materna* into two dialects: one thought fit for the refinements of Art and Love, the other considered appropriate only for the gross business of every day. But various early vernacular poets, from William to Dante, had been there first, creating out of *chutzpah* what the scholars would feel obliged to justify in the name of *pudeur*.

That initial *chutzpah,* however, soon ran out, even for the poets that followed; and, in any case, those who wrote in the "glorified" or subholy tongues could no longer pretend to speak—or even to translate, render at a second remove—the Word of God, but only the words of men, which is to say, of themselves. And though with the passage of centuries and the replacement of the Church by the University as the chief instrument of education, certain humanistic texts began to seem more orthodox than heretical, finally canonical, they constituted no real Scriptures; only pseudo-Scriptures sufficient unto that pseudo-Cult, the Art Religion according to Matthew Arnold—or, in its revised American form, the Great Books Religion according to Robert Hutchins or the New Critics.

It is characteristic of aggravated *pudeur* that it tries to disguise even itself, pretending it is piety rather than mere bashfulness and shame and guilt; but the hermetic tradition, as it has passed from Arnold to Eliot to Leavis and Cleanth Brooks, is revealed finally as mere gentility, i.e., *pudeur* utterly bereft of *chutzpah*. To be sure, our early twentieth-century gentility is more highfalutin, perhaps, than the middlebrow gentility practiced in the middle of the last by, say, Longfellow; but it is equally hollow in its pretenses, redeeming neither language nor souls. Without an adequate faith to justify it, any venture at defining a canonical literature, like any attempt to separate a sacred language from a profane is revealed as one more spasm prompted by the castrating shame which has been haunting Western Art ever since the first Western artist set out to sing of sex and the "I." The chill that freezes the marrow of worshippers at the altars of High Art is not just the cold that possesses all empty churches, but the zero weather of the Eternal Winter, which sets a new generation of readers to shivering even in our superheated classrooms and libraries.

What, then, is to be done? To deliver the Waste Land of our Universities from shame-ridden sterility, shall we swing to the opposite pole—woo the Eternal Summer in which the Bacchae can dance in the *Aula Magna,* as well as on the lonely peaks; and all distinctions of high and low, kith and kind will be melted away in ecstasy? There is always conceivable at least, if never quite possible, a third way eloquently described by Lévi-Strauss in the inaugural lecture quoted earlier.

> In the face of the two possibilities which might seduce the imagination—an eternal summer or a winter just as eternal, the former licentious to the point of corruption, the latter pure to the point of sterility—man must resign himself to choosing equilibrium and the periodicity of the seasonal rhythm. In the natural order, the latter fulfils the same function which is fulfilled in society by the exchange of women in marriage and the ex-

change of words in conversation, when these are practiced with
the frank intention of communicating, that is to say, without
trickery or perversity, and above all, without hidden motives.

"Never quite possible," I have written (and I return in conclusion to the first person, since that is what I must remain in the silence, the blank space that follows my final phrase), thinking of
communal life or even the psychic life of the individual; since in the
first "perversity" is the rule, and in the second "hidden motives"
are inevitable; and "equilibrium," therefore, in either case merely a
wish, a fantasy, a dream. Perhaps this has not always been so; but
certainly it is so now, when we no longer possess—in a world of
air-conditioning and travel so rapid that summer and winter are
hours rather than months apart—the inescapable pattern of "perio-
dicity" provided by the "seasonal rhythm" of the natural year.

Only in poems does man create the balance which Lévi-Strauss
proposes and himself momentarily achieves on the page: in the use
of language we call "literature," and which, keeping faith with both
poles of our ambivalence, relies upon "trickery" and is shaped by
motives hidden even from ourselves. Only at the moment of becoming a poet can the anthropologist create the ideal community, the
perfect marriage which as a citizen, lover, father, even teacher he
inevitably betrays; and he does so, ironically enough, by abandoning or transcending "the frank intention of communicating" in
favor of the deviousness of the artist.

It therefore matters not at all whether the poet is asserting the
possibility or impossibility of "equilibrium" in the world outside his
text. His success in the world depends not on his declared allegiance, but on his undeclared ambivalence. And this is equally true
if, like Lévi-Strauss, he is projecting the hope of such a solution, or,
like Euripides in *The Bacchae,* singing its inevitable failure: the terror of repression, the terror of release not complementing or fulfill-
ing each other, but only destroying turn and turn about those who
have committed themselves either way. In either case, the end is
irony; since in the former the equilibrium achieved in the lecture
hall is lost in the streets, and in the latter the equilibrium achieved
in the theater belies the message which is its occasion. Yet the second kind of irony seems more appropriate to a historical moment in

which not the long-term goals for which we demonstrate, but the short-lived Demonstration itself seems to provide all the community we shall ever have; and in which, therefore, not marriage—as for Lévi-Strauss—but the Orgy—as for the Bacchae themselves—becomes the key Utopian image.

Small wonder, then, that *The Bacchae* of Euripides is currently on everyone's mind, as it has been continually on mine in these reflections on the seasons of the soul; that it among the surviving plays of the Attic theater occupies for us the central position held for our immediate predecessors by Sophocles' *Oedipus Rex.* At one point, during the past year, there were playing in the major theaters of the Western world, five new adaptations, free, faithful, naked, clothed, of that play; and as I walk the corridors of my own university, I see posted on the wall just outside our graduate student lounge (itself recently decorated in the course of a "mind-fuck" with painted slogans: FEMINISM LIVES. EAT SHIT. FAR FUCKIN' OUT. TOUCH ME FEEL ME HEAL ME) a casting call for the chorus of yet another production of the same play.

Clearly not every director who revives the *Bacchae,* in this time of a major shift from the tyranny of *pudeur* to the reign of *chutzpah,* realizes that Euripides is singing the inevitable failure as well as the inevitable resurgence of the dream of Eternal Summer. But all are aware that we have somehow used up the personal-psychological myth of the son who knows all the answers, yet does not know he has murdered his father and married his mother; and stand in the need of one more communal-political: the archetypal tale of the repressive son who, in the name of the *Polis,* the State, imprisons his mother's God, only to be ripped apart by her hands for the sake of her *Thiasos,* the Pack that worships her God on the hills.

Both myths seem at a glance equally absurd, yet the first has proved amenable to rational analysis from Aristotle to Freud; while the second stubbornly resists rationalization, leading only to non-wisdom, the ironic tag with which Euripides chose to end this last of his plays, as he had earlier at least three others.

> What we look for does not come to pass;
> The God finds a way for what we did not foresee.
> Such was the end of this story

It is less elegant as well as less hopeful than Lévi-Strauss's peroration: an absolute conclusion beyond which nothing can be imagined, an ending which consumes all beginnings, past and to come. But perhaps it is, by that token, closer than any prophecy to the true myth of our history, though whether more *chutzpahdik* or more *pudique* I am at a loss to say.

Buffalo, New York
—1969

Index

143